V.I.E.W.
Bryan Jacobs

Chapter 1

The shape of a young man was outlined thinly in the dark; bathed in the artificial light of the single screen fixed to the ceiling above the bed. His form still seemed juvenile, too small for the grown adult he had become, but he didn't care about being the strongest or biggest. Owen Lyonne had always been more interested in mental exercises.

The room around him was modest. A few posters of his favourite musicians decorated the walls, along with a tacky, ornate cuckoo clock that chimed the hour by releasing a flock of rare birds. The size of the flock represented the hour so that, for instance; at six o'clock, six birds of paradise would fly around the room.

Beside the huge bookshelf, where Owen kept all of his archived media, the light pollution gave the sky a mustard sheen above the Los Angeles skyline. Remediated skyscrapers could be seen through the window, silhouetted by the moon. Patches of new material stood out against the original infrastructure of the giant buildings that had been salvaged from ruin during the chaos of two decades prior.

On the desk across the room, glowing in the light of the city, sat a stubby little cactus with a flower about to bloom. The rest of the desk's surface was scattered with files and documents, so there was only just enough empty space for work to be possible. Owen hadn't been working though, tonight his thoughts were elsewhere. He lay in bed on his back, eyes staring through his glasses at the progression of images on the display above.

To an observer, the room would have been completely silent, except for the sound of Owen's breathing. There were no speakers in his room to output the audio for the feed. They weren't necessary. Instead, the sounds for the images could be directly transmitted to the cochlear implants freshly installed deep within Owen's ear canal. He could hear everything as if he was really there. Owen had held off upgrades as long as possible but it was almost to the point that he was being ridiculed in public for his normalcy. It had been about time for him to jump onto the augmentation bandwagon.

The scene on the monitor in front of Owen was familiar; a trendy, high-end loft apartment in Toronto. On his last visits, it had been a well-organized home but tonight the huge room had become a raucous dancehall. The high ceilings in the apartment were pulsing with psychedelic imagery that moved to the music from speakers embedded in incandescent orbs, which floated majestically around the room flashing neon colours just over the guest's heads. Vibrant crimson gave way to stunning emeralds with golden shots of chantreuse accent. Each transition of colour was designed to complement the music and the fractal shapes on the ceiling to create a connected sense of ambience in the venue.

All this was conceived and actualized by Owen's closest childhood friend Shayne Riche. A talented artist, he had spent days designing the layout for this event. Shayne had a reputation for throwing amazingly extravagant parties and this was one of his better. He stood by the door greeting the wave of friends that had just arrived, ensuring that no one got in that wasn't invited.

Shayne made a good bouncer. With his muscular frame, he never let a situation get out of control. He had been augmenting himself for years now, with nearly all of his senses having been digitally upgraded. He had gotten a full suite of audio and video augments as well as musculature enhancements, where piezo-elastic fibres were woven into his sinews and ligaments to massively increase his strength and stamina. These smart fibres in his tissues responded to conducting electrical current by pulling tight, assisting Shayne's movements, making him stronger and able to move by using less caloric energy.

Once these latest guests had passed Shayne's security clearance, he was satisfied that enough people had shown up for the party to really get started. It was time to activate the rest of his decorations' functions. Using only his thoughts, he sent the command; able to do so because of the neuro-augmentative treatments he had started getting just recently.

The lights dimmed as the music changed beat. The shapes on the ceiling began to bulge out from the roof as if they were going to drip off onto the dancefloor. Simultaneously, the floating spheres began to move with a purpose, synchronizing their flight while they too began to contort their shapes to match the rest of the scene. From the orbs, shot sharp, metallic points in all directions, resembling a drop of ferrofluid responding to a magnetic field. The choreographed procession of shapes and colours built to a climax in time with the music as the crowd below watched in awe.

Even with the amount of detail that Shayne had put into the setting for his party, all of Owen's attention was on the beautiful brunette that he'd been making eyes with since she'd walked in the room. To him she seemed as if to be half heartedly feigning modesty, in a digitally rendered high-cut top and full length leggings. Owen's sprite decided to take his first chance to talk to her. Owen watched from his condo in LA as the screen replayed their conversation at the party earlier that evening. Or was this live?

She said her name was Matilda Seiler, or Mati, as she wanted him to call her. A Belgian from the capital Brussels, she had come with a guy, Sarmad from Dubai, that Shayne knew. Checking his

Telexistence profile, Owen found that his projected sprite had logged these experiences to the database only 15 minutes ago. It seemed to him like this event would be going all night.

Owen understood his sprite's initial attraction to Mati. The programs that controlled its actions had been captivated by the way she had chosen to present herself that evening. Her style had been interpreted by Owen's Telexistence algorithms to mean that she had exquisite taste and that she had wanted to get noticed. Owen knew that didn't mean the real Mati would be anything like the sprite she had chosen to send.

As he watched their representatives get acquainted, Owen skipped ahead through the feed to see if she had permitted him access to her contact information. Not yet. They didn't get that far before they decided that the dancefloor had filled up enough for them to go join in.

It wasn't unusual for people to be guarded about who they gave their information to over the network. Telexistence allowed anyone to be represented anyway they wanted, wherever they could imagine. So it was always best to make sure that you knew who it was you were talking to before you discussed anything too intimate. Owen would have to hope that he got another chance to speak with Mati later, since there wouldn't be much talking on the dance floor.

Having caught up to the live feed from the

party, Owen began to wonder how his other active sprites might be doing. There wouldn't be much interesting to see from the party until after he and Mati had finished dancing. Watching only made Owen frustrated that he couldn't really be there. With a flick of his wrist Owen switched the feed on his screen from the party in Toronto to a concert that he was also attending in Vancouver. He didn't even have to get up off his bed to make the trip.

The live music screamed in through Owen's audio implants as the images in front of him changed. An amelodic symphony of notes in hyper-treble and ultrabass were emitted from an array of ancient analog instruments, retrofitted with custom distorters and synthesizers. Owen saw his sprite's perspective of the full orchestra of musicians, each with their own unique, custom-made noise machine, whining to its own beat. The Vogue Theatre was the perfect place for this show to have been scheduled. The acoustic resonance of its arched fixtures only added to the depth and richness of the melodies.

The real Owen reached out his hands towards the screen above his bed, as if to try and pull it towards him. In response, the monitor dislodged itself from the ceiling and began to hover downward to give him a better look at what his sprite was seeing. As the screen approached, it appeared to get larger. It stopped its descent only a foot or so above Owen's face giving him the equivalent of a 47 inch display. The definition was so crisp that the objects on the screen seemed like they should be falling out of the plane onto Owen's bed. It looked like a window into another world that existed just behind the real one.

This was made possible by the VIEWer headset that Owen wore. The glasses, that sat high on Owen's cheekbones, were sleek, thick rimmed and handsome, with all of their functionality hidden within their stylish exterior. When Owen looked through the lenses, the feather-weight pico-projectors embedded in the frames created any of the myriad of images that might be required to create a fully digitized experience.

The headset used accelerometer technology to create three dimensional renderings of digital objects by displaying continuously changing two dimensional images. The angle that the object was being observed from was detected and this information was used to adjust the image appropriately to sustain a hologram. This technology was ubiquitous across every urban centre on the globe and a majority of all objects that individuals in these areas interacted with on a day to day basis had been digitized on the VIEW network.

Owen wanted to know what other people thought about the performance his sprite was recording for him. He left the audio feed from the concert going but he reached through the screen to bring up his media interface. The screen dissolved instantly into an aether of pixels and what appeared to be a newspaper reformed in Owen's hands.

He sat up in bed and began to read through the interface that he had just made manifest. He had chosen the nostalgic newspaper skin for his media interface and it rendered every detail of the simulated publication down to leaving virtual ink stains on Owen's fingertips. The only major differences between the interface and a real newspaper were the videos in place of still images and the live text that continuously updated.

He flipped through his personalized media interface. It had been his to customize since the age of twelve, so he knew exactly where to find the reviews he was looking for. Not in the Creations section. That was where all of the newest digital objects and materials were announced. Maybe you might find a different skin for your sprite there or a new AIR game to play. Passed the Social section; that was full of updates and messages from all of Owen's contacts.

He finally came to the Entertainment section. It listed all the newest art and other media that might be of interest, as well as all the live events that he might want to attend; in person or otherwise. He looked for the article that had convinced him to go to this show tonight.

Before opening up to the live reviews that were being added, Owen cast a quick glance at a blank spot on his wall. Right where he looked a new screen appeared that brought him back to the video feed from Shayne's party.

Owen's sprite was still on the dancefloor. It seemed like it had managed to get pretty close to Mati. The virtually represented dancers at the party allowed their forms to be passed through by the other guests, making more room for each other to move. There might have been more than 200 people there but you could dance as if there were only twenty. This produced an eerie scene of blurred, spectral figures moving through one another. It looked like a collage of bodies on the dancefloor.

The music in his ears changed, still from the concert, so Owen turned his head to another blank spot on his wall. This made another display to show him the video from that feed. A triplet of musicians had broken from the orchestra and began exchanging turns leading their collaborative solo. Their instrument constructs were some of the most striking that Owen had seen. A cello's body had countless buttons down the neck and a subwoofer imbedded in the frame, allowing the instrumentalist to make some of the most mesmerizing bass tones imaginable.

Beside this was a wireframe oboe that, while still using a reed, had a visible interior composed of an extremely complex system of tubes and ducts. These knots changed the sounds in a vast assortment of ways. The last performer was using a traditional theremin that she had patched into a network of distortion and loop pedals. Pretty standard compared to the other instruments, but she played it with a unique magnificence.

As he listened to the song they made together, Owen looked back at his interface. In the Entertainment section he saw live reviews of this concert being continuously updated, along with articles for other concerts that he had chosen not to project to.

An infinite amount of digitized experiences were being uploaded to catalog every perspective of these events and most of them were freely accessible to anyone on the network. Someone on the network barely needed to send sprites to events anymore to get a feeling of having been to them. Going only ensured that your perspective was part of the collective digital experience.

Most of the reviews for tonight's show were extremely positive. There were some in attendance that didn't quite have the capacity to understand the beauty of this particularly challenging genre. Post-retro orchestra was a wild force and it really all fell on the conductor to bring everything together.

Owen gestured towards the reviews for the show he was attending, so that he could get a feeling for what the consensus was about tonight's conductor; Psynota. He was the reason that Owen had chosen to go to this show in Vancouver. Owen had been following his career for years. He appreciated the variety of musicians that Psynota chose to work with and how he was able to balance the entire spectrum of those diverse styles.

Owen's gesture caused his interface's display configuration to instantly transform as he became wrapped in a large cylinder of words. All of the letters and punctuation that was contained in the reviews for tonight's show became the walls of the tube that surrounded him. Many of the reviews were about specific members of the orchestra, most of whom were famous artists in their own right. Owen wasn't interested in these articles, he wanted to filter them out so that he would only get results about the conductor.

"Search term: Psynota," Owen spoke to no one, still sitting in his bed. Immediately a three dimensional representation of the conductor appeared in front of him, in the center of the cylinder. He appeared tall and thin, in an animated costume that made him appear to look like an elemental creature of flickering purple and black fire. This outfit, of course, was only the skin which the performer had chosen for tonight's performance. As with most private celebrities of the day, his true form was not known outside his closest friends and relatives. The alternative would be to have constant security escorts and no escape from the sprites of overly sentimental fans.

The figure of Psynota was surrounded by his mixing table, a custom design, covered in uncountable buttons and knobs that changed the music in minutely specific ways. It was impossible to imagine how anyone could have learned to master this setup, even in multiple lifetimes.

Most of the messages on the cylinder display's wall disappeared and were replaced with ones that better matched Owen's query. Specific reviews about Psynota's performance flooded his field of view. One that had stood out to Owen read, "The sounds of

Psynota's performance are like the cries of some beautifully hideous sea creature, lamenting the death of its infant child."

For some reason, that sombre imagery resonated in Owen's mind, so he saved it as a favorite on his profile. The rest of the other reviews he saw were along those same lines, but less poetic. For the most part they were all so positive that Owen decided he had to add an opinion of his own.

"Psynota's attention to every detail of his show creates the perfect expression of his specific style of discordant orchestration." He continued to gush, "His blending of such extreme differences between the musicians he chooses always makes for an exquisitely unique experience."

As soon as the comment was logged to the network, Owen instantly begun getting replies from his friends that were jealous of having missed the show. Owen again made to grab his newspaper interface by reaching through the display, dissolving the cylinder of comments around him.

He found himself back in his bed with his interface in front of him, still listening to the sounds of the concert. He changed his mind, holding the simulated newsprint up in front of him at arm's length. Owen released and it stayed floating there, becoming a screen bringing him back to the video feed of the party.

The dancing was still happening. A small

group had finished and gone back to sit on the couches. It was barely noticeable but the feed had become partially distorted. Owen knew that some of his sprite's inebriation filter algorithms had kicked in. This meant that his projection was picking up on deviations in his friends' behaviours, the ones that were really there. Owen was interested in what kind of fun his friends were getting into tonight.

He studied the display to see if he could figure out what filters had been activated. He saw blurred outlines and a small video delay which was obviously the alcohol filter. Big whoop!

Owen also noticed that the colours were skewed, making them appear brighter. There seemed to be an accentuating focus on any physical sensations. Tiny visible sparks appeared whenever the projection touched things, like rubbing Mati's holographic leg while they danced. It seemed as though Shayne had broken out the hard stuff tonight. Owen had wondered what they were doing while he and Mati had been talking earlier.

Owen's sprite at the party spotted Shayne dancing near him and Mati. Shayne's body was still encompassed in a virtual skin to modify his outward appearance even though he was not digitally rendered himself. He was really only wearing a pair of boxers; the bare minimum necessary in his warm apartment. The outfit he wanted displayed was added to the visual information of the observer by their network device.

Shayne was seen to be wearing a neon blue button down that seemed to be made of transparent plastic. Through it, the argyle patterns of oversized suspenders over his bare chest could be seen. His eyes were whited out, which Shayne thought hid his visual augments while still hinting at the upgrades. The microphones that replaced his ears were still fully visible and his muscles were outlined with silver weaving to show off the rest of his enhancements. He couldn't cover all his implants or else someone might think he was ashamed of them.

Aside from that his appearance was pretty plain compared to some of the eccentric ensembles that some of the guests had chosen. A few of the ladies had coordinated their outfits in a faerie theme, with fluorescent butterfly wings and skimpy outfits made of torn animal print fabrics. One of the girls had obviously spent extra time programming her outfit, her silver-blue wings flapped while she danced and she wore a dazzling sapphire tiara over her golden hair.

The faeries had found an oddly amazing looking guy covered with flagellated tentacles. The appendages replaced his hair, came out of his face and protruded at key spots near his joints that best accentuated his dancing. The tentacles all moved independently to the music as if the were all controlled by their own seperate brains. These were the costumes that stood out the most as far as Shayne was concerned. Everyone had outdone themselves in preparing for the event though.

As he continued to dance in the sea of projected partiers, Shayne bounced from real bodied guest to real bodied guest trying out new dance partners and playing the good host. Everyone understood that the sprites on the dancefloor were mostly unmanned right now and they were just documenting the events unfold. This meant that they could just be ignored, unless one talked to you. Their owners were likely occupied elsewhere anyway, until their sprite's interactive functions were re-enabled once they finished dancing.

Instead of trying to get his attention, Owen sent Shayne an instant message. "Great party," the Owen in the bed typed to his friend. A keyboard appeared instantly in front of him as Owen's hands began to type. "The decorations that you designed are amazing. Everybody's so tripped out! You really outdid yourself this time buddy."

"Hey man, glad your having fun." Shayne replied without gesturing, since he was able to use the neural keyboard he'd just had installed. "These visuals are nothing really. It was easy to program once I figured out the look I was going for. How's that concert you're co-attending?"

"It's so great! Psynota is even better at structuring his blends live. I'm not sure if it would be the right kind of music for this party though, haha."

"Ya, you have always liked that crazy post-retro shit. There's no beat. Not really good for dancing." Immediately, he also sends, "Woohoo! This is a blast!"

The moment Shayne sent that last message the music at the party hit a beat that made all the guest cheer. The same classic house beats that had been popular since the late 1980-90's were still pretty much what played in the clubs now. Only a few innovations in the types of sounds they were able to incorporate had been made in decades. The driving bass was exactly the rhythm that you wanted if a party was going to go all night. Everyone had really started to feel whatever they'd taken now. Owen decided it seemed like a good time for him to sneak off to take a shower.

As Owen got up off his bed, he removed his VIEWer headset putting it down on the desk. Without his glasses the world changed. Gone were the posters and cuckoo clock. All that was left was the neutral grey that everything real was painted. That way it didn't clash with the digital overlays. The bookcase and the cactus had vanished too and the space where the window had been was filled in by wall. All of the clutter on the desk disappeared as well, so Owen had no trouble finding space to put down his glasses.

All of those object had been holographically produced by the headset, which Owen still required since he hadn't gone in for optical augments yet. It wasn't that Owen had anything against augments or the company, he didn't see the need to improve upon what nature gave us. Those opinions didn't sit too well with people anymore though and Owen succamb to the social pressures when he had gotten his audio implants. He was just sick of people asking him why he didn't have any upgrades.

Owen was quick in the shower, mostly focusing on cleaning his healing ears to help the process along. He had managed to avoid an infection, so far. Augmentation was addictive, the same way people before digital objects had been addicted to tattoos and piercings. After the VIEW Cooperation took over, body modification fell out of style, along with most everything else that could be replicated by digital objects. Until augments were developed.

Now, most people had several implants and it was seen as suspicious and almost anti-social to not have embraced the technology. It was generally thought the only people that were skeptical enough of technological advancement to not have opted in yet were the ruralites, who refused to live in the urban centres.

Hurrying back to his room, Owen's body still glistened with beads of water. In all of his excitement to get back to the feed from the party, he hadn't finished drying himself off completely. It was a good thing that his VIEWer headset was new enough to be waterproof, since his hair soaked them as he replaced the frames on his face.

Knowing that they were being worn by sensing Owen's body heat, the headset immediately booted up and loaded all of the holograms that had been active in his room. The glasses used tiny video cameras near the lenses to identify the location that the user found themselves in. This way the same objects could be experienced by any other user in the same place, as long as they had appropriate permission.

Once the contents of his room had rematerialized, Owen brought up a couple screens to catch him up on what his sprites had been upto while he was away. He was hungry though and wanted a snack before going to bed, so he set his monitors on mobile mode. This meant that as he walked out of his room, the monitors travelled with him; staying at the fixed distance Owen had preset.

One screen took Owen back to his sprite at Shayne's party. He had finally decided to go take a seat on one of the big couches and Mati was right behind him. They had been dancing for over an hour straight, inebriation filters in overdrive, and now they were ready take a break. The other feed that was supposed to be from the concert, was blank. His sprite had disabled itself after the concert had ended. So, Owen rewound the feed to show him all that he had missed.

While that loaded, Owen moved to bring up his terminal module so that he could give his sprite at the party instructions. The terminal was just a floating keyboard and a smaller command prompt monitor so that Owen could see the code that he typed. He wanted to try and get Mati to give him permission to contact her and he wanted access to her profile so that he could see what she looked like in person. He wrote this, still walking down the hallway towards the kitchen.

The walls in the hallway were programmed to display family portraits that moved and waved as Owen walked by. Owen didn't care much for them. He despised having his deceased mother stare at him everytime he went passed. His dad, Carter, insisted on having them. He said that they always had to remember her in every way they could.

Owen walked passed his father's room. He could see light still peeking out from under the door and knew that his dad was still awake. He hadn't come out for dinner that evening and had missed work that day too. Owen knew not to worry though, he had been doing this a lot lately. If he hadn't come out to eat something by the time Owen got up in the morning then it might be time to worry. It was just best to leave him alone for now.

As Owen walked passed a digitally rendered palm tree, one of his monitors had to quickly dodge out of the way to avoid a collision. Both the holographic objects could have merely went through one another. Since Owen and Carter were both master programmers. the more complicated version was all that would suffice for them. Carter had spent weeks figuring out the most elegant commands to execute that specific function.

Owen arrived in the kitchen just as the video of the concert finale was ready to be played back. He paused the video to allow himself to go to the fridge to get some fruit and a beer. He had to walk to the counter and put his drink down so that he could have a hand free to restart the show.

Pre-choreographed laser flourishes and impossibly intricate pyrotechnics beautified the scene in front of him as the magnified forms of flowers grew and bloomed. The great display of petals hovered over the stringed instrumental section while a tempest's gale grew from over the woodwinds.

In the centre of the stage, Psynora's form had grown and combined with the storm visualizations; making an amazing black tornado. This had all been accompanied by a melody that had begun almost as a ballad, slowly incorporating harsher tones as the imagery developed.

Now at its apex, purple bolts of lightning were let off by the dark cyclone. This always joined a staccato crash from the percussion section. Owen was blown away by what he was seeing. So much so that he ended up walking into his bedroom door, distracted by the wondrous performance.

The show ended with a standing ovation. As Owen finished eating his snack, he decided that it was time for him to go to bed. Shayne's party would be going on all night and Owen had to be into the lab early the next day. There had been a few snags on his project recently and it had been forcing him to work extra.

Instead of bugging Shayne at the party, Owen sent him a message for later wishing him a good night. He told Shayne to give him a call in the morning, also adding a reminder that they had planned on working on their characters in the Medieval Fantasy AIR channel the next night. After he was finished sending the message to his friend, Owen started his nightly bedtime ritual.

Owen placed his hand on his chest and said, "Load: Sprite 2." A blue glow was made to be emitted from his hand and he pointed it at the floor in front of him. The light shot out from his hand like a bullet, directly at the spot he had been pointing to. From the floor where it hit, a copy of Owen appeared. Owen reengaged his touch control interface and started typing out the code for its instructions.

When completed, Owen turned away from his doppelganger and went to get into his bed. He left his VIEWer headset on. He had gotten used to sleeping in his glasses and they had been designed not to break if he rolled onto them during the night. As Owen got comfortable, his projection took off flying straight through the ceiling.

Owen sat in his bed with his legs under the blankets and looked around the room. All of his walls were now giant screens, showing him the feed of what this new projection was seeing on it's flight. This version of him was already well above the tallest buildings in the city. It looked down and saw the bright lights of the urban centre and the total darkness of the rural lands.

The sprite kept climbing up and up, above the

Earth. The scene was blocked momentarily as his sight was obscured while passing through a thick cloud. Higher and higher. He looked up now, out towards the stars. Flying passed the industrial waste dumps of the satellite orbitals, there was finally a clear view of the vast emptiness of space.

Back in his room Owen laid down to sleep, comforted by the look of the walls around him. They were all encompassed in a deep black hugh, accompanied by the added speckled twinkling of live starlight. It was as if he'd ridden his bed out of the atmosphere.

Chapter 2

At the usual 6:45 a.m. for workdays, the digital clock application that Owen used to wake himself went off. Of course, the ringing sound from the clock was generated from Owen's ear implants. He didn't have to worry about waking anyone else up. The clock interface had a red, glowing read-out of the numbers for the time. They floated, just in reach, beside his bed.

He flailed his arm at the hovering digits, to disable the alarm as he sat up in bed. The room was already bright with the first rays of sun, just starting to catch the reflections off of the enormous glass buildings through the simulated window. He liked to leave himself plenty of time in the mornings to catch-up on all the updates from the sprites that he had left active overnight.

There were only two for him to review, so it wasn't going to take very long this morning. The sprite that he had sent up into space had spent the night studying the weather and satellite data in order to give Owen a precisely accurate meteorological forecast. It contained a minute by minute prediction of temperature, wind speed and precipitation for the whole city. Owen studied the forecast, looking for the areas that he would go during the day. It was going to be pretty nice out, warm enough that he wouldn't need a heavy coat. Even in LA, it could get chilly in February.

Owen closed the forecast application and disabled the sprite that had compiled it for him. He then switched to the feed from the sprite that spent the night at Shayne's party. Just glancing at the amount of video that had been added, Owen could tell that the party had only just ended. The last update went out just two hours ago. With the time difference, it would have been almost 8:00 a.m. in Toronto.

Almost all of the footage that had been logged since Owen went to sleep was of his sprite and Mati. The last frame was of their two forms tangled together cuddling on one of the couches just before Shayne shut the party down completely. Again, Owen checked to see if Mati had granted him permission to see some of the more private aspects of her profile.

He found that he had more access than last time he checked, but he still couldn't see pictures of what she really looked like. He could see her location and got excited when he noticed that she was in LA. Also accessible were her personal interests, as well as who she was closest friends with. He could even send her unfiltered private messages at anytime. Owen hoped that meant there was still a chance to get to know her better in the future.

Satisfied with his virtual representatives' evening's work, Owen got out of bed and began to get dressed. The clothes he chose were really just basic thermal garments. They all came in the same standard grey of everything else that underlaid the digital reality. These were only meant to provide the material warmth he would need, based on the temperature read-outs that his weather forecast application had provided. Once he was adequately covered for his body's physical needs, it was time to choose the outfit he wanted that day.

Owen walked towards an open space on the wall while gesturing to open his fashion interface. In front of him a full body mirror materialized, adorned with an antique gothic frame that seemed to be made of charcoal coloured wrought iron. Looking at himself through the mirror, Owen saw how others would see him through their VIEW network devices. The choices of outfits available were endless and there was really no social etiquette anymore for what to wear when. Owen was on his way into work today and he didn't like it when people's outfits were overly distracting when he was trying to be productive.

He picked a century old style right out of a 1950s mobster game, with a black pinstripe jacket and navy pants. His undershirt matched his pants and his tie was a crimson red. He finished the outfit with a pinstriped fedora to match his jacket and some slick, black and white wingtip shoes. This may have been over the top at some points in history but was tame and professional by today's standards.

After his game of dress-up, Owen had already been awake for over an hour. That left him enough time to have some breakfast and still be able to meet with his security detail to be escorted to work. He stopped by the washroom on his way to the kitchen, to quickly relieve himself and brush his teeth. Some things would never be able to be replicated digitally. In the kitchen, Owen found his father just pouring his first cup of coffee.

"Ah. Good morning Owen," Carter greeted his son, looking up from his cup. "Did you sleep well?"

"Ya, I slept fine. How about you?" Owen replied, as his father failed to notice the cup he was pouring spill over. "Did you get any sleep at all?"

His father was still seen to be in the same outfit that he had been projecting the last time Owen saw him. He hadn't bothered changing his fashion layer and Owen doubted he had changed the material layer underneath either. Carter Lyonne appeared to wear a whimsical patchwork suit and top hat that seemed as if they were intended for the costume of a vagabond clown. Mr. Lyonne's face beneath the hat was deeply drawn with wrinkles and the circles under his eyes were nearly dark enough to be mistaken for bruises.

"I probably dozed off for a bit at some point." Carter suddenly noticed the mess he had made and found a cloth to wipe up. "I'm not too sure though. I really don't feel well either way. Do you think you might be able to cover for me at work again today?"

"Again dad? Why do you keep working all night? Have you been taking the sleeping aid that the medic gave you?" Owen whined with a fleeting concern. This was becoming an almost daily routine. Carter had already missed more than half his days of work this month and Owen had been the one picking up the slack.

Carter didn't bat an eye before going into the same explanation that he had given Owen every other morning this had happened. "I've told you before, its extremely stressful to be the Lead Developer on the company's flagship project. The system we're making is one of the most technical pieces of software that the company has ever tried to produce and I'm the one responsible for getting it done. Is it odd that I can't sleep when we still haven't even figured out a data compression technique that will manage to keep the volume of data manageable? Our current methods are compromising the data's resolution, making us lose critical details."

Owen wished that he could believe that his father was telling the truth. If it was just the project that was getting to Carter then he wouldn't feel so worried. His dad didn't want to talk about what he was really doing all night. It would only start a fight if Owen bothered to bring it up.

"What's the point of all this research if it

prevents you from making it into work?" Owen chose to entertain his father's version of things. "You have to be able to apply what you learn to the project. But, if you can't make it in again. I'll cover for you." He knew to give up. Ultimately, he was aware that in this condition his father wouldn't be cf any use at work anyway. It would just be better for him to stay put at home. Hopefully he would actually sleep.

Still, Owen couldn't help trying to evoke some guilt in his father for the increased workload he was being forced to take on. "You know you were supposed to be interviewing for Joseph's replacement today, right? That should be the Lead Developer's job."

At this point the senior Lyonne's disappointment in himself became palpable, "I'm sorry to put that on you son. You've been such a good Assistant Lead on this project." He walked over to where Owen was sitting and gave his son a pat on the shoulder.

Owen had to stop himself from rolling his eyes. "Assistant to who?" He only thought, having already achieved his minor victory.

As Carter walked back to where he had been sitting, he sent a message out to the members of the project's development team. He told them that he wouldn't be able to make it in again, but he was thankful that Owen had once more agreed to take on the role of Lead Developer for that day.

Immediately after he sent out the message, Owen started getting alerts about private replies that the team members had been sending him. No one was surprised to learn that the senior Lyonne would be absent again. Some wondered how much longer the company would put up with him before they just officially made Owen the lead, permanently.

The rest of breakfast was eaten in almost complete silence, with the odd tidbit of advice from Carter to Owen. Instructions were offered about what to look for in the applicants during the interview process. These conversations were all brief though, since Owen was already well versed in each of the interview procedures that his dad brought up. Carter had, in fact, been absent for the process of hiring the last five project members to the team. Leaving Owen to have to fill in.

At around a quarter to nine o'clock, the buzzer for the door to their apartment rang. Owen messaged the company security personnel he knew were waiting outside that he was ready to go and that his father would not be joining them. Usually they would be able to just go down and greet the guards by the transport but that was not the case if someone was staying behind. As they had learned when Carter had previously missed work, it meant the guards would have to come up to the apartment to confirm his father's status visually before they would be able leave without him. This precaution was necessary to ensure that Carter was not missing, injured or in any other form of distress.

These stringent security measures had been put in place because of the company's interest in seeing this particular project completed. Unfortunately this special treatment also made the team working on the project an attractive and probable target for anti-company terrorists to attack.

Many that chose to live outside the cities did so because of moral or ideological objections to becoming an employee of the company, as was required for all urban citizens. The Neoluddites were the main organization of radicalized ruralites that intended to destroy the VIEW Cooperation and the hold the company had on the urban centres.

There had recently been a surprising and dramatic increase in the number of disappearances or defections by employees, especially in the Los Angeles Urban Region. The project Owen was on had seen five vacancies in the last two months, with most of the employees vanishing without a trace. Those that they did find were certainly not the lucky ones. This was the reason for all the interviews that Owen had been conducting lately.

These disappearances signalled to the company that this project had clearly been targeted specifically by the Neoluddite resistance. Protecting the key members of the production team had been made a top priority to ensure the progression of their work.

Owen said goodbye to his father, and followed the guards to the transport vehicle. The project site was not too far from their apartment, but the company had still sent an armoured truck to take the Lyonnes to work. Designed to resist explosive attacks and bullet fire, the bulky vehicle was made from a repurposed money truck, from the time of national currencies. The emblem of the VIEW Cooperation had been animated to jump across the onyx slate surface of the truck, marking it as property of the company.

One of the escorts opened the back door for Owen to get in, then joined his partner in the front of the cab. Once alone inside the closed cubicle that served as the passenger bay of the truck, Owen's VIEWer made the walls dissolve all around him. Without them, what was outside could be seen in every direction.

The apartment the company had provided for Owen and his father was in an affluent area of the city, usually reserved for those considered to be the greatest contributors to the growth of the company. Most of the neighbours were either other top product developers or politicians representing one of the parties that wrestled over control of the company. A presidential estate was down the street for whenever the sitting leader of the global cooperation was on business in town.

The company didn't have the resources to rebuild most of the cities after it gained secure control from the rural forces. Most of the nicest residences were refurbished relics from before the collapse. There was only a limited number of these luxury accommodations and they were reserved for high performing individuals that got results that benefitted the company and in turn, every employee on the planet.

Average employees lived in comfortable compartmentalized habitations made with material efficiency as their priority. This meant that there wasn't much in the way of actual facilities; most with shared toilets and scheduled bathing. That didn't matter much, since the occupants still had full access to the VIEW network to satisfy their every need for entertainment.

Walking their pets down the sidewalk, Owen saw two older, retired women, that looked as if they must have been almost 50. They exemplified the gaudy excesses of the post-material age, with their over the top costumes and exotic varieties of artificial cats. One lady was walking a purple lion with an orange mane, while the other walked what actually appeared to be a glowing neon pink panther. The ladies themselves were projected to be wearing frilly, baroque-themed costumes in colours to match their feline companions. They were likely ex-top employees that had earned tenure in this neighbourhood by their contributions.

It was common for people to get only 20 years of work for the company at most, as there was really not much work to go around. Most people spent the remainder of their time experiencing the world that VIEW had to offer; going to events, playing virtual games on the AIR channels, or getting to know new people using the Telexistence system. It worked well for the company because they had a never ending supply of loyal beta-testers. They just had to be sure to supply the basic living essentials for the urbanites.

As the truck began to move, Owen wondered if Shayne was up yet. It was passed noon in Toronto and even if he was up until morning, Shayne was usually a quick sleeper after a night of stimulants. Owen checked to see if Shayne was online so that they could talk. He did this by saying, "Status: Shayne Riche," into his headset.

In his ears a moment later, Owen's audio implants replied, "Status: Active." He was awake. Owen tried to see if he was in any condition for a call.

Owen instructed his VIEWer to, "Call: Shayne Riche." With these words the VIEWer responded by projecting, on the seat beside Owen, a blue hominoid figure with no distinguishing features whatsoever. It emitted the sound of the ringing alerts that were being sent to Shayne to try and capture his attention. With each ring the edges of the blue form would vibrate violently, like the pulsing line on an electrocardiogram monitor. After the fourth ring, Shayne answered the call and the golem immediately transformed to represent him.

"Ugh, good morning," Shayne groaned, as he answered the Telexistence chat call. He looked rough. It seemed like he probably hadn't slept at all. His hair, that had been meticulously styled the night before, had been ravaged by countless head messages through the night. The rosy colour in his cheeks, that usually gave him a healthy glow, was gone; leaving his face pale with exhaustion. He was still wearing the same shorts that he had been wearing the night before, but his shirt was no longer there.

"It's afternoon there already Shayne, isn't it?" Owen replied cheekily.

"Fuck you buddy," Shayne chuckled. "You missed some of the best parts of the party after you went to sleep. Such a great time. You get a chance to catch up on what your sprite did for you yet?"

"Ya most of it. Seems like I did pretty well with this new girl I met named Mati. Did you meet her? She's from Belgium and said that she knew your friend from work, Sarmad."

"There were so many people there man, I don't know." Shayne was not in the mood to think very hard.

"The one that I was with when you and I had our little chat on the dancefloor."

"Oh ya," His memory jogged. "I think Sarmad introduced me to her when they first got here. She had a cute, naughty librarian look going. A little bland for the party though. Still, seems like she might be your type. Did you get to see what she really looks like?"

"Not yet, but I did manage to get messaging

permission. So it's not hopeless. Not to mention our sprites ended up cuddling the whole night." Owen smiled with a sense of accomplishment.

"That's my boy!" Shayne said giving his friend a congratulatory high five. Even though Shayne wasn't really there, they still made the manoeuvre without a problem. Owen's arm served as the reference point for the high five and when his arm was fully extended the chat program brought Shayne's holographic arm to meet it. This way there was no sloppy graphics bugs where their arms would pass through one another. The same process was duplicated on Shayne's side so that the effect was simultaneous. The system even provided the soundtrack for the clap.

Immediately after, a pedestrian they passed on the sidewalk outside the truck caught Shayne's eye. "Woah! People are ridiculous out west, hey? I mean, we aren't even on a fantasy AIR channel."

The person was seen to be dressed as an elegant centaur creature covered in tribal tattoos. His equine half had the markings of a zebra with a flowing rainbow striped tail. He was wearing a pink bow tie and top hat to match. The hat was pulled back just far enough so as not to hide the singularly magnificent, golden horn that protruded from his unicorn forehead.

"That's just too much," Shayne moved on. quickly losing interest in the man's flamboyant attire. "So, you still want to game tonight? Medieval Fantasy, right?"

"Ya that'd be fun. If you think you can make it." Owen knew that personally he wouldn't be able to do anything after a night like Shayne had. "I should be online after dinner. I want to see if I can get my character that new fireball spell tonight."

"Ya, I should be able to nap this afternoon while you're at work." Shayne had always been able to burn the candle at both ends. "You'd never make it passed that Dragon by yourself anyway. Your mage has pretty much no stamina."

"Well excuse me Mr. Warrior class. It takes way more courage to go into battle without wearing Heavy Armour." Both friends started laughing.

They had been playing immersive games together on the VIEW network for years. Owen usually preferred AIR channels that involved character building and role play, while Shayne usually opted for shoot'em up style or racing games. Another company acronym, AIR was short for Augmented, Immersive Reality and was the general term to describe the way that other worlds could be rendered on the VIEW network.

"I think there's a new axe in that dungeon for my character anyway, so I will be there for sure." Shayne said, resuming their conversation. "After the dungeon you think you might want to try that new Zombie Apocolypse channel that just launched?"

"Oh yeah, I just read an article about that yesterday. Sounds fun, kind of like an action RPG world. No character classes though, just a big sandbox. I like things a little more structured than that. I'd be willing to give it a try though, I hear it gets real scary in the difficult areas."

"Okay, good. I better go get some sleep, sounds like it's going to be a long night of gaming"

"Alright, sounds good. You look like you really need the sleep anyway." The friends finished their goodbyes and Shayne's form vanished from sight as he disconnected the call.

Their chat had lasted nearly the entire trip from Owen's apartment to work. His lab was located at the VIEW L.A. Headquarters, which used to serve as the old UCLA campuses. If you saw the campus without your VIEW network device it would look almost identical to how it was in 2014. But through his glasses, Owen looked upon a giant golden cube whose base encompassed the entirety of what was once the campus grounds.

All the old buildings were still intact on the ground levels at the base of the cube. They were for the on-location employees to complete their work in a material environment. The rest of the virtual structure was for the benefit of all the numerous projected employees conducting their research on site. The buildings had virtual additions on higher levels that were only accessible by sprites. These upper floors stretched all the way up to the top of the cube, getting wider as the rose so that they completely filled the internal volume of the shape outside.

The structure stood as a monument to the VIEW Cooperation's enormity. It was visible from most of the city. Owen was very glad that the window in his room at home faced the opposite direction or he would have to turn the window off if he wanted to sleep. He liked that the moonlight shined into his room instead of the blinding light that radiated off of the Headquarters. The golden cube was emblazoned on each side with the name of the company in giant letters that sprawled across the entire width of the cube and came at least a third of the way down. The letters changed colour at a set interval, fading between a deep crimson and a regal purple.

As the armoured vehicle approached, the light from the Headquarters began to get so bright that Owen reengaged the opacity of the cabin walls. He understood that the company was attempting to instill confidence in the urban citizens with this marvel, but Owen thought it was an eyesore. What's worse is that with all the possible structures that they had available to choose from, the company had picked this same Headquarter design for every major metropolitan centre that it governed.

In the New York Urban Region, the View Headquarters had encompassed the blocks around the Empire State building. Owen was under the impression that the golden cubes looked better surrounded by skyscrapers in a downtown core than they did away from the city center. Without the ordered framework of urban sprawl to cradle the shape's artificial precision, it looked like an awkward pimple on a more wild and natural landscape.

Owen felt the truck stop as it arrived at the gate to the entrance of the facility. They would have to clear a security checkpoint before they would be allowed to pass. Instead of coming inside the cabin to check Owen's identity, a sprite was sent in to question him. The projection of a new guard, that must have been the one manning the checkpoint, appeared in the cabin with Owen.

"Please confirm the medium of your presence on campus today. Material or digital?" The female guard had no softness in her voice. She spoke with a coarse urgency that implied she thought she was deserved respect. Owen was to obey her and abide by her authority. He was fine with that. Owen wanted to avoid finding out what happened to those that upset her.

"Material. I'm really here."

"Please just answer the question sir. Vocalize your name aloud and disengage any facial projections that you may have activated, please." Owen had gone through this procedure everyday on his way to work but never had the pleasure of dealing with this guard before. She was particularly unpleasant, even though she was only doing her job. Security was almost as important to the company as maintaining the VIEW system itself. That was because they already knew full well what the Neoluddites were capable of.

"Owen Lyonne," he obeyed.

"Voice and facial recognition confirmed. Have a nice day at work Mr. Lyonne." With that, the guard vanished leaving Owen alone in the cabin. He felt the truck resume moving as it continued into the compound. Owen spent the rest of his ride reviewing some more of the footage from Shayne's party. He was interested to find out what else he had missed happening the night before.

Chapter 3

Ten Years Earlier: 2041 A.D. - New York Urban Region

Seymour Riche looked out at the finest hardware development facility in the world and the deserving research team, hard at work inside. They were under his supervision and the project all of them worked on was, primarily, of his design. There had been help from a few of the smartest minds Seymour had ever met, that just so happened to belong to some of the most important individuals in his life. He counted himself as lucky to be able to work with people he loved on a project he was absolutely passionate about.

The lab was stocked with all the gear that might possibly be required for any job that their engineers could foreseeably encounter. A mishmash of material and digital objects, each tool had earned its place in the lab based on its specific function. Digital objects were always the preference since they were essentially free, excluding the cost to maintain the VIEW network. Not that these things were measured in dollars anymore.

Hudson, Seymour's wife, was busy in the clean room with a few technicians. She was attempting to grow the nanochip crystal circuits that would serve as the picoprocessor unit on the device they were developing. They were attempting to build computers that were able to be surgically implanted into a user's body. These nanocrystal circuits were their best chance at getting the processing power they needed while maintaining a biologically inert system.

Just outside the sterile room, at their desks, sat the team's senior software developers, Carter and Avery Lyonne. They were working out the algorithms that they would use to interface the device with a person's sensory organs. They had to translate the neural messages that the body naturally used and write programs that would allow information to move between the processor and the user. Avery often joked that perhaps 'patient' would have been a better term than 'user'.

The goal was to be able to create the VIEW network experience without the use of peripheral devices. All the hardware was to be installed inside a user's tissues to allow them to directly interact with the digital world. It remained to be seen how popular the technology would end up being but for now it was still an interesting proof of concept.

These four, the Riches and Lyonnes, made up the team's executive committee. They were in charge of making all decisions about how time and resources should be properly allocated. This made them directly responsible for the completion of the project and the company had them keep detailed records of all of their prototypes and trials.

They had several other people on the team, mostly doing data entry and assisting with fabrication. This project had been proven to be plausible by the collaborative effort of this group of old friends. They all agreed that Seymour had been the one to design the initial concepts however, so it was him that was the one to present the idea to the company.

Mr. Riche left his team to their tasks, having plenty of his own duties left to do. They were more than competent enough to supervise themselves. He turned towards the testing area that had been converted into a makeshift surgical theatre. On the table, sedated and prepared for operation, was the live pig to be used as a test subject in today's trial.

Seymour washed his hands and put on his mask and gloves. An assistant was already in the room with a tray of stainless steel medical equipment on a wheeled cart next to the table. Beside the utensils sat the new prototype optical casings. They were meant to contain the current model of the visual enhancing biological augments. The casings held the device in place within the user's skull.

The optical implants were designed to replace the eye in the socket. High definition cameras were magnitudes better at seeing than the natural retina could ever be. The microcomputer within the device added virtual holograms from the VIEW network to the footage automatically. The unit used neuro-digital connections to allow the information generated from the device to be communicated to the user's brain so that the user was unable to unplug from the network, ever.

This was only a preliminary test of the biocompatibility of the current working design of the device. The pig would have the casing implanted to determine the likeliness of rejection or infection before moving onto human trials. Since this was the fourth generation of casing prototype, Seymour made quick work of installing the implant in the swine's face. The previous models had either been proven to be of inefficient shape or the materials that they were made of had not been well tolerated by the test subject's immune system. Hopefully this would be the last pig that would have to be sacrificed for the progression of the company, at least on this project.

With the device securely inserted into the socket of the subject animal's eye, Seymour went back to the washing station to clean up from the grisly task. The pig would be put under close observation to make sure that the new addition was taking. An assistant got started cleaning and sanitizing the test room.

Walking back into the main area, Seymour immediately saw that Hudson had finished her work in the clean room and was typing her report into the terminal at her desk.

"Finishing up for the day hunny?" Seymour asked checking in on his wife.

"Just writing up the results of this trial. I think we have a replicable technique for getting the crystals to form the circuit matrix." Hudson answered in the matter of fact way that she always had when it came to work.

"That's wonderful news! Good job. Have you determined if the process would scale up to handle larger markets? Would we be able to produce millions of units if we had to?" The couple were good at maintaining a professional working relationship.

"Should be. We might need to convince the company to build more clean rooms. Or find a way to compress the production area so we can do more with the space we have, but there's no reason it wouldn't work. It's fast too, we made a dozen chips just today."

"Okay. Sounds like you've done great work. I'll read the rest in your report when you've finished. I just have to go do my paperwork. Should be done in the next half hour or so."

"Ya, I'll just wait with the Lyonne's if I finish before you. We're still going over to their house for dinner tonight, right? We might as well all take the same transport over."

Seymour gave his wife a big thumbs up and

said, "I'll just go confirm with them."

He went over to the software workstation to see how his friends' work was progressing. Seymour arrived to find the still cheerful and young Carter Lyonne talking with an intern about his work. It seemed the new hire was not meeting Carter's expectations. Their conversation finished up just as Seymour got there.

"Is everything alright?" Seymour asked his friend, as the intern walked briskly out of the room. His pace had increased substantially when he saw the Project Lead approaching.

"For the most part. We're progressing along steadily but," Carter hesitated. "I'm beginning to suspect there may be inconsistencies in that new interns credentials."

Carter said this with caution. Perjury on an employment application was a serious offence. Skills and education records were maintained and administered centrally by the VIEW Cooperation. This meant that any educational fraud would have to be the action of a sophisticated group that could hack the VIEW Data Archives.

"Wow, are you sure?" Seymour replied in shock. "That's a large accusation to be making lightly."

"I know. It's not something that I would ever joke about. I just don't have enough evidence yet to make a cohesive enough case to bring it forward to the company." A cold seriousness overcame Carter's face that let Seymour know his friend was truly concerned about this.

"What makes you think he falsified his credentials?"

"I think that's something that we should discuss later tonight." Carter knew that the company had a habit of monitoring the conversations of its researchers. All use of the VIEW network on company property was subject to minor surveillance. However, it was rare for any action to be taken against employees based on these records alone. The company's strategy was to allow people to feel free to speak their mind, but still keep records of what happened in case something was needed to be referred to later.

"Oh, good. So does that mean we are still on for dinner at your place tonight?" Asked Seymour, "I was just coming over here to confirm that with you for Hudson."

"Yes, I'm pretty sure Avery ordered servings for all of you. We should all head over to the apartment together in the same transport when we finish here. The boys were headed there after their lessons to play some virtual games together."

"I hope Owen does his studying before they waste the whole night in alternate realities. His mechanics classes aren't going so well."

"He has other skills. Owen is better with his mind like his father. He's going to make a great software developer one day. Not to mention, Shayne can give him a hand with engineering. He's a natural at it. Maybe Owen could help him with programming in exchange? That's where Shayne's been having the most trouble"

"I'm sure both boys would like that. You're right though, they both have their talents. The other night Owen showed me an inefficiency with a program that Avery and I were writing. I was shocked that he was able to even comprehend such advanced logic"

"They sure take after their parents, don't they? Ok, I've just got to write up my report of our progress for today. The company demands we run a tight operation. Hudson is going to wait for me in the reception with you guys after she finishes up her work, then we can all leave together when I'm done."

"Okay, give us a heads up before you're finished and we'll call the transport so it's ready for us. Avery and I are just finishing up our daily reports now."

Seymour went to his desk to get started on his clerical work. He had an assistant check on the hog that he had mutilated to make sure that it was still breathing. It turned out the pig was doing fine. It had come out of anesthesia and seemed to be in significantly less pain than the previous subjects had been. That was a good sign. Seymour decided that he was still going to prescribe a cocktail of immunosuppressive medication to lessen the likelihood of rejection and some antibiotics to fend off infection.

After he finished for the day, Seymour met up with his wife and best friends to go catch their ride home. The transport took them from the VIEW New York Headquarters in what was once Midtown Manhattan, down 5th Ave to the Lyonne's apartment near 65th and Madison, a stones throw from the Central Natural Zone. When they got up to the apartment, the couples found their sons, Shayne and Owen, running around the living room shooting at virtually projected enemy mercenaries on a War Zone AIR channel. The pieces of a broken vase laid uncleaned by the mantle of the fireplace, one of the boys had obviously knocked it over without noticing.

"Owen," Carter yelled upon seeing the vase. "What have we told you about playing the AIR channels in the living room? How many times do I have to tell you? We still have material objects in here, and they can be broken." The vase had once served as an urn for Carter's father's ashes. The ashes themselves had been stored in a biological preserve, under company orders. The vase only served as a memento to the previous transience of life.

"Sorry dad, I didn't even know that we had come into the living room, these games are getting so good at augmenting the world around you that you can't even tell where you really are anymore. I think

I'll have to reconfigure the games range so that it wont let us come in here."

Owen was an unathletic 15 year old. His pale, spotted complexion betrayed him, revealing how much time he had been spending on the VIEW network. The wearable peripherals were nowhere near as sleek as they would become with time. Carter couldn't even remember what colour his son's eyes were, not having seen his son without his headset in years.

"Alright, let me know if you need help configuring that range. Please just clean up that mess." Carter pointed to the broken vase. He then turned his attention to the mantle and by engaging his interface he recreated a digital version of the vase, from memory, to replace the broken one.

"After that, it's time to go washup for dinner." He instructed the boys.

Their meals were delivered by a company food van. They had been prepared in the VIEW kitchens as per the orders that had been placed through their interfaces for that day. Carter had ordered Surf and Turf, while Seymour had ordered Cornish Hen, Avery and Hudson had gotten a Cobb Salad to share and the boys had ordered a medium Cheese Pizza.

They all sat at the table enjoying their respective meals. The adults made conversation while the kids watched movies on a screen that hovered above the table. The mothers attempted, unsuccessfully, to get the sons to try a bit of their salad to get some greens into the boys diet.

When they finished Hudson and Avery went to the Central Natural Zone with their sons so that they could play their virtual games outside without worrying about destroying the house. The large area was the remnants of the old Central Park, but most of it had been unkempt for decades and overgrown. The small Gamer's Park in the middle of the CNZ, where the women took the boys to play, was all that had been reclaimed from the wilderness. Luckily there weren't any large predators around to worry about.

Seymour and Carter stayed behind and had drinks in Carter's study. This gave them the chance to discuss the situation from work in private.

"So Carter," began Seymour, getting directly to business, "tell me what you know about this new intern."

"Well, the name he applied with is Roman Kraner. I think it was you that hired him. Supposedly he's fresh out of the academy, but it's almost as if his training was at least five years out of date. All of the code and algorithms that he has written don't use nearly as modern a proficiency as was indicated during his application." Second guessing himself, Carter does concede, "There is a possibility that he just does not do well with the modern techniques and is using the skills that he feels most confident with."

"No skilled programmer would prefer those ancient relics." Seymour wouldn't stand for outdated work being utilized on his project.

"The new techniques work so much better. I think you're right to be skeptical." Seymour reassures his friend of his concerns. "What do you need to investigate this matter further Carter?"

The Lyonne patriarch took a moment to think about how he might be able to prove his allegations. "I could go down to the academy that he claimed to have graduated from. If his mentor is still employed there, maybe he can remember whether the intern that we hired is the same person as the student who completed their training there."

"That seems like it would be proof enough. You can have the day away from the lab tomorrow to investigate, but make sure that you don't tip the intern off to your suspicions. If he's is really guilty of this, who knows what else he might be capable of." Seymour warned his friend, "Just get enough proof so that we can hand him over to the company. We can't know what this supposed Mr. Kraner might do if we approached him with this."

"Of course Seymour." Carter completely agreed with his friend and supervisor, "The company has specially trained people to deal with these situations."

The two men refreshed their drinks as their conversation changed to the latest sports results.

Their wives and children returned home within the hour and the Riche's left shortly after that to go home before it got too late.

Later that night, Carter explained to Avery that he had been given the day away from the lab to visit a local academy. He did not tell his wife the real reason for his excursion. Instead, Carter made up an excuse about an old teacher friend that had asked him to come in, to guest lecture a class about bio-digital interfaces.

Avery was surprised by how little notice that Seymour had given Carter. She complained about having to manage the interns all by herself but Carter told her the whole thing had been on his initiative. He gave his wife an earful about how Seymour had been very generous to give him the time off with such short notice. Carter finished by apologizing for forgetting to mention all this to her beforehand.

This had been enough to satisfy Avery's curiosity. She and her husband sent Owen to bed, following not too far behind themselves.

When they woke up the next morning, the Lyonne family ate their breakfast together. As was their usual custom, after they'd finished preparing for their day. Carter made sure to call into the company early to have them send an extra transport, explaining that he had permission to have an alternative destination.

This was not very well received by the

company bureaucrats. They had to contact Seymour at home before they were able to process the request for travel variance. After verifying Seymour's approval though, the company happily obliged sending three transports to take each Lyonne to their individualized destinations.

Owen was first off towards class, followed closely by Avery. Carter gave his wife a deep embrace, wishing her a pleasant day in the lab and telling her that he would see her that evening. He might have held her longer if he knew what that day were to bring.

After seeing off his wife, Carter loaded himself into the last transport. He confirmed that it was destined for SoftTech Academy, where Roman Kraner had apparently learned to write code. It was about a 45 minute journey to the academy that was situated on the outskirts of the city. On the way, Carter looked up the mentor that Roman had referenced on his application and checked if he was still at the academy. He was able to make an appointment to meet with the professor in person first thing before his morning class.

After he was done with that, Carter still had time to look in on a sprite that he had sent into work with Avery. It was to procedurally help her with any mundane tasks that might need to be done around the lab. Of course the projection could only do work that didn't require it to interact with a material object. Their job was optimizing the translation algorithms that were to allow the implanted devices to communicate with the wearers conscious mind. That meant there was lots of coding to be done and that didn't require the ability to touch things.

Carter's transport finally drove through the gates of the SoftTech Academy, letting him out when it arrived at the main administration building. He told the clerk at the desk that he was there to meet with Professor Lund to discuss an old student of his. The lady gave Carter instructions to get to his office and gave him a picture of the professor so that he would recognize him.

Upon seeing the image of his face, Carter remembered that he had spoken to Professor Lund via chat call a few weeks earlier to verify Roman's transcripts. The instructor had offered a raving recommendation about the ex-pupils purported capabilities. This had proven not to be the case with the Roman Kraner that had come to be employed on Carter's development team. He meant to find out how such a mistake could be made.

Professor Christopher Lund was a tenured member of SoftTech Academy's faculty. He had been teaching students advanced programming and algorithm design for over a decade. He had taught dozens of the company's past most prominent developers. Carter had probably hired several of his students before. the academy was a renowned place to hire from. This was one of the reasons that he was so surprised by Roman Kraner's sub-par performance at work and now he had to come to the professor with these concerns.

Carter found Professor Lund in the secondary conference room waiting to begin their meeting. He was an old man with wild, grey hair. It struck Carter immediately that he wasn't wearing a headset device. Behind him Carter was amazed to see a materially real computer, straight out of the 2020s. It was a laptop notebook that had been upgraded so that it could connect to the VIEW network. Professor Lund must have been so old when the digital object revolution happened that he never adjusted to the change. There was something to be said about the way things felt in your hand, Carter mused.

"So glad that you were able to make time to see me Professor Lund," Carter greeted his fellow colleague. "Sorry to have to bother you with something like this."

"Not at all Carter, and call me Chris." Christopher Lund had never been one for maintaining formalities. "Besides, if your suspicions turn out to be true, it's really my ass that's on the line here. My assistant's already filled me in. A previous student of mine isn't performing up to standards and that reflects poorly on me"

"No Chris, I'm sure that your curriculum is up to snuff. I've never had a problem with any other pupil from this school. Maybe this one was just extra sneaky about how he cheated. One's always gonna slip through eventually. We just got to make sure that it isn't anything more insidious than that." Carter was trying to reassure the professor, he hadn't mentioned the extent of his suspicions to the assistant. "Just tell me what you remember about Roman Kraner while he was a student with you."

"Well, it's like I told you. The kid that I remember was quick as a whip. He never needed anything explained twice. Instant master of all the latest techniques. I think he was top of the class, although that was a pretty competitive year, that Suzanna Hughner almost beat him on the final if I remember right."

"That doesn't fit the Roman I know at all. He's still using techniques from 4 or 5 years ago. It's really slowing down our work."

"Oh? Well that's not the Roman I recommended. He had only just started programming, he got a scholarship from the games circuit. The kid worked his way up through the Strategy Games League, he was sure a master of logic. I taught him every piece of code that he knew though and that was all the newest techniques."

"We are definitely talking about different people then." Carter said with confidence. "Do you have a file picture of the Roman Kraner that attended your class?"

Professor Lund shared the file image with Carter over the network. The image he received looked nothing like the intern he had hired. Who was that in the lab with his wife and best friends? What could he possibly want?

There was no doubt anymore that the Roman Kraner currently working at the Main Facility was not the same one that graduated from SoftTech Academy. A feral rage built up inside of Carter, compelling him to act in order to protect his loved ones.

Remembering the advice that Seymour had given him, Carter ignored his gut instinct to play the hero and confront the imposter. Instead, he followed protocol and called into the company Security Forces tip line to report his findings. He would rather have called the fake Roman and tell him that he was found out. He didn't want that punk thinking he was going to get away with this. That was stupid though.

Carter had to calm down and get his emotions in check. It was impossible to tell how the phony Roman would respond and tipping him off only gave him the opportunity to get away. It was better to let the authorities handle this, they were trained for these situations.

His call went through and he was confronted with a sprite of a nice looking young security receptionist with a very high pitched voice and the kind of chipper personality that made you want to vomit. She tried to start the conversation with small talk about the day and weather but Carter stopped her, stressing the importance of the reason for his call. She was not at all impressed by his abrupt urgency, but she was quick to be convinced once Carter told her he wanted to report a possible fraudulent employee.

"How on Earth would someone be able to lie about their education? Those records have the most encrypted security software that the company has developed." Carter couldn't help but feel that this woman was a little bit ditsy.

He went on to explaining that he was an executive on the Biological Augmentation Project and he had an abundance of evidence that suggested that the new intern on his development team was not who he said he was. This meant that he must have had connections to a large network of countersecurity specialists that had helped him to infiltrate the hiring process.

As the gravity of the situation became more clear, the receptionist took on an entirely different persona. She began to move with the strict precision of a seasoned veteran back on the frontlines and her perkiness dissolved into an aura of disciplined action.

She ordered him to upload all of his evidence to the network so that she may pass all of the details of the case to her superiors immediately. This was something that could not be acted on soon enough. They had to begin strategizing how to best remove the imposter from the lab without letting him escape or potentially causing anyone harm. Seymour's ride was ready so he set his evidence to upload for the clerk and began to make his way back towards downtown.

The ride was long to begin with; but under the circumstances, Carter's tension was going to make it agonizingly slow. He wanted to call his wife, to tell her to get out of the lab. Roman could be dangerous and he didn't like the idea of her being anywhere near him. If he did that though, he risked tipping Roman off and letting him get away, or worse. He couldn't even risk talking to Avery. In his current state she would hear in his voice that something was wrong. All there was to do was wait.

He tried to pass the time filling out the paperwork to request a new intern to replace the one he was about to lose. He couldn't upload the application until after the security forces had moved in on Roman since that too risked some sort of way to tip him off. Carter sent a sprite to a favorite golf course, just outside of Palm Springs, to play a few holes and try to calm down. He was so distracted that he couldn't do better than a double bogey.

Too soon, Carter felt the transport decelerate as it left the freeway. They should still have been at least another twenty minutes away from the exit for the company's New York Headquarters.

"What's going on? This isn't the way to the VIEW Campus," Carter enquired to his militarized driver.

"We just got orders from the Central Security Authority. We're to reroute our course to the nearest secure location." Carter was confused by this. "A significant threat has emerged. We need to get you to a safe place."

Something must have happened. "What sort of significant threat? Was there an attack?"

"There was no more information in the update. I'm sure the company will issue a broadcast any moment to inform people how to keep safe. Please just remain calm sir and allow us to ensure your protection."

A deep dread began swelling inside Carter's stomach. What were the chances that something should happen within an hour of him reporting a fraudulent employee? This could be no coincidence. Something had gone wrong when the security forces had closed in on the imposter Mr. Kraner. Carter had no way to confirm these suspicions; his calls to the facility were left unanswered.

Before too long, just as the guard had said, the company did release an official broadcast. It was worse than Carter could have imagined. The entire Primary Laboratory at the New York Headquarters had been reduced to rubble by a massive explosion. It seemed that the security forces received a tip that a member of the research team working there had falsified their education records. Upon further investigation at his residence, the body of the real Roman Kraner, was found cut into pieces and neatly kept in the refrigerator's freezer. Volumes of files detailing the progress of the Bioaugmentation project were also found, as well as lists of employees involved on the project with their contact information and addresses.

The insurgent had been working for months to find a way onto the development team. Once he got a job at the facility he began collecting information that may have been of any use to the terrorist groups that he worked for. At the same time he began to smuggle covert explosive devices, in pieces; rebuilding them on site and planting them at critical places around the lab. It seemed his mission had been to collect as much information about the project as was available. When he was done, or if he was found out, he was to inflict the most damage possible and cause as many casualties as he could. Unfortunately, he had been very successful.

The imposter fell victim to his own success, but still managed to take dozens of employees with him. The damage to the Headquarters was extensive and images of black smoke billowing out of the top of the golden cube accompanied the company's broadcast. Finally a list of missing or dead employees was displayed. Carter began to weep as he read the names of his best friends and wife on the list. Seymour and Hudson had already been confirmed deceased but Avery's body hadn't been recovered yet. Just like that, all his most cherished relationships had vanished. Despair and bitter loneliness began to creep into his mind as he realized the he would now be raising his son on his own.

Chapter 4

Present Day: 2051 - Los Angeles Urban District

The bulky armoured vehicle rolled to a stop outside of the Main Research Facility of the VIEW Los Angeles Headquarters. The building was the premier Software development centre for the entire company. It supplied the teams that worked inside with all of the best possible equipment and resources.

Since it was currently the company's primary objective to complete the project that Owen and his team were working on, they were given the most well-stocked space in the Main Facility to conduct their operations. Owen took for granted the caliber of equipment that he had access to each day.

There was fierce competition for the company's favour between development teams. They all hoped that any success that got noticed would yield an equipment upgrade or better labspace. Bitter rivalries boiled between research teams as resources were allocated by political priority, always leaving someone with the short end of the stick.

The lucky ones on the other hand, enjoyed comfortable progress on their projects. Any of their whims were met without hesitation, magnifying the contribution they made to the company. This compounded to create a stable cushion for the nearly noble executive class of researchers. The rest were doomed to tasks that would most certainly be made redundant by the time they were done. The functions of their devices would be better performed by some other technology that had been developed by a team given preferential treatment.

Owen stepped out of the transport onto the uneven sidewalk outside of the Main Facility. It was no more than five stories tall physically, but the digitally rendered extension made it seem as if to stretch the whole way to the top of the golden cube. Those floors were unreachable if you were flesh and bone. You had to send a sprite up if you had business on the virtual floors.

From inside, the golden cube seemed even more immense than it had from the exterior. Owen looked back from where he stood, towards the cube's entrance and could see some of the dozens of similarly enhanced buildings that made up the campus complex. The cube's golden glow was nowhere near as intense once you were inside the compound. The scenery outside was visible through the perimeter walls. Only tinted slightly as if looking through sunglasses. The cube functioned as an enormous one-way window. Those inside could look out, but no one connected to the network could look in.

Owen climbed the stairs to the top level that he could go to in person. His team was working out of Laboratory 1, lovingly referred to as the Main Facility's Penthouse. The biggest, best stocked software development site on the planet. Most programmers only dreamed about setting foot inside.

Owen entered the lab through the heavy metal doors that served to maintain the security shield around it. The walls of the room were made to take a nuclear strike without failing. At the same time it made the room sound proof and impervious to electromagnetic imaging devices. An armed guard outside was the only one that could unlock the door. To even approach the door without the proper clearance was enough to be incarcerated.

He was technically the boss today, so Owen was immediately greeted with a coffee. One of the team's junior assistants handed it to him, gleefully. High achieving students from local academies were given the opportunity to participate in top level development projects the company was working. This provided the chance for the pupils to gain firsthand experience on how products were created.

Most of the time, however, these junior assistants were used as food servers or errand runners. They received very little actual experience.

The students were usually happy to do it though, hoping to get to know high profile researchers that could recommend them for positions with the company in the future.

Owen made his way passed all of the different workstations, towards the office that he shared with his father. It was the executive suite inside of Laboratory 1, reserved for only the best of the best. Most desks sat empty at the moment due to a minor snag that the project had encountered recently. The team needed a new Data Compression Specialist. The last one, Joseph Pellon, had disappeared almost two weeks ago.

The project was not running at full capacity without the position filled. The company had decided that they had waited long enough to replace him. It was not yet known if he had been hurt or captured by extremist, had fled in fear or if he had defected. Regardless, the odds were not on his side. In the past few years the survival rate for missing persons after the twelfth day was exactly zero.

While arriving at his desk. Owen opened his day scheduler program. The notebook interface informed him that he had arrived well before the first interview of the day. Owen decided he had enough time to take a look around the lab before his first appointment arrived. Very few things could be done at this point since by now almost every task had hit a data wall.

Each part of the project produced a geyser of

information. It all needed to be compressed and translated so that the interconnected parts of the system could function. This meant they needed help compressing how the information was structured so that it could be stored more efficiently and be accessed easier by other subprocesses.

The project that Owen and his team had been charged to complete was called the OtherObserver Project. The goal was to allow projected versions of an individual to act as separate primary observers for their shared identity. They wanted to create a quantumly unified identity by entangling the agency of the user with that of their sprites.

The very idea was only possible due to invention of the new neural augmentative technologies. The concept was extremely advanced. Using the neural augments the user would be able to live update between their mind and each of their projections, theoretically allowing them to simultaneously experience multiple perspectives. Carter had been made Lead Developer after he had proven the concept was plausible. He was then able to get the project prioritized by convincing the company that it was the key to the future of their digital network technology.

The only major thing still happening in the lab that day for Owen to look in on were the human trials. He went over to the test area, where the experimenters were probing their subject to observe the current prototype's performance. The researchers had found volunteers that had wanted to have exclusive access to the latest advances in neural augmentation.

The selected subjects were of the type that would welcome attempts to surgically implant digital interfaces directly into their cerebral cortexes. Fortunately for the subjects, no incisions were required. Although many would have still volunteered anyway. They had been fine signing waivers that even covered procedures that might involve drilling a one inch hole into the base of their skull. So long as enough other people were volunteering too. People tended just to want to fit in.

The administration of the VIEW Cooperation makes it a point to try and not maim their employees. The neural augmentation technology was currently being administered by retroviral genetic therapy. The smart vectors targeted specific neuronal cells in the volunteer's brain. These neurons were coerced by the specifically bioengineered viruses into expressing proteins that had functional sites that were able to interact with parts of the electromagnetic spectrum.

The antenna proteins communicated with the radio waves that transmitted the wireless digital communication signals that carried the VIEW network. Different cells responded to slightly different frequencies to create patterns of activity in the brain that simulated real experiences. The same mechanism in reverse allowed the user to send information back to the network. This technique was able to connect that volunteer's mind directly into the virtual world.

Presently, the system could only complete relatively simple tasks. Limited mostly to typing or executing simple commands. It would still be some time before the neural augments would be capable of creating immersive digital optical and audible experiences.

The research trial that Owen watched now was attempting to combine the auditory experiences of a volunteer and one of their sprites. The subject and their projection were to be listening to two entirely different songs simultaneously, in entirely different locations.

"Alright miss, we are ready to begin the trial now." The researcher's soothing demeanour did not undermine the authority of her labcoat. What may have sounded like courtesy in her voice was entirely a concern with preserving the data she was there to collect. "Shall we proceed?"

The young female subject nodded to the experimenter. She responded by flicking her wrist, causing a slow classical ballad to come over the room's speakers. It could be assumed that the gesture had started music playing for the unseen sprite as well.

"Alright," the researcher continued, "now if you could kindly start up the OtherObserver software that we've installed for you. There should be a shortcut icon on the home screen of your neural interface"

"Ya, I feel it." The subject used the natural term that people with neural augments had come to. She described what using her neuronal upgrades was like. "Just need a second for the program to load."

While they waited for the system to boot-up inside the subjects brain, there was nothing visible happening from Owen's perspective. Not really all that much to be observing even though these events were history in the making.

"Okay, it's running." The young lady said without even changing the expression on her face.

"That's good. Please describe what you feel. We'll be recording everything you say. We really have no other way of evaluating this device so please be as descriptive as possible. If you could?"

"Whoa. This is the weirdest feeling I think I have ever experienced," the volunteer said to the researcher with wonder.

"I can tell my projection is listening to a different song. I can't hear it but I know it." The way she said, "know" was accentuated to emphasize how intense the knowledge was.

"I feel what song it's listening to. I know how far into the song it is, but I can't hear it. Not in my ears. Its definitely my sprite's experience, but I don't really understand how I'm not there. I think I can even feel a draft in the room that it's in." There is a definite hint of confusion in her voice.

Seeing this made Owen feel proud to be a part of this particular development team. This project was really going to do wonderful things for the people of the urban centres, even if Owen didn't quite understand how. That was for the company to figure out. Owen felt a connection to how his parents must have felt a decade before, on the cusp of developing bioaugmentation technology.

Owen heard an intern call, "Mr. Lyonne, the first applicant is ready for you."

"Okay, sit them in the interview room, I'll be right there." He answered. Owen stopped at his office to quickly brush up on a few details about the person waiting for him. It solidified the impression that the interviewer had authority if they went into the meeting acting like they already knew everything about the potential hire.

He spent the rest of the morning with applicant after applicant, asking each of them the standardized questions that he had gotten approved by the company's administrators. All of those interviewed were astonishing according to their profiles. Most had been top of their class and some were already team leads on other prominent company projects. Why shouldn't they prefer the esteem that came with being on this particular team instead?

Most applicants were only able to send a

sprite to the interview, not having been able to make the journey in person. Some were even hoping to work from satellite offices but Owen was put off by the idea. He didn't want the team to become disjointed by not being in physical proximity to one another. He thought that it was more conducive to the team's productivity for them to really all be in the same place together. That way all of their attention was on the work at hand.

Even though the company had complete authority over what questions Owen asked during the interview, the ultimate decision for who got the position was his to make. All of the questions that he had requested had been approved anyway. The company had just added a couple of questions relating to the applicant's urban loyalty or about their general thoughts on ruralites and Neoluddites. These were intended to be security questions, designed to prevent the possibility of a rebel insurgent or saboteur getting in.

Owen was certain that they were far too obvious. Any self respecting Neoluddite should be ashamed if they fell for these glaring attempts to lead them into incriminating themselves. The company did have the capability to biometrically polygraph the applicants, through Owen's headset, as a back-up. In Owen's mind, a proper spy should even be able to fake that too.

By lunch Owen had gotten through five interviews. Already, he had no idea how he was going to be able to narrow down the field. It was a pretty sure thing that the second applicant was going to be rejected by the company. He had some pretty robust experience in food technology and had spent a lot of his time doing research in the Subrural agricultural areas. That would probably be too much of a security risk for the company leadership to be willing to take on.

The Subrurians were technically employees of the VIEW Cooperation, but they had their own government and their own laws. The people in those areas had resisted the elure of Telexistence and digital objects for various moral, or ethical, reasons. It was widely suspected that anti-company ideas were propagated amongst some of the more influential groups. The relationship between the Subrurians and Urbanites had never exactly been trusting.

There were still supposed to be three more applicants to get through after lunch. Owen hated how long this day was dragging on. He made his way to the cafeteria to get himself something to eat. A freshly grilled Reuben Sandwich was ready for him when he got there, as per the order that he had placed beforehand. He took his meal back to his office and decided that while he ate he would send a sprite around to the other laboratories in the Main Facility.

It was always interesting to see what else the company was working on and the administration encouraged researchers to check in on each others work. This was supposed to reduce errors by opening research up to peer review. It was also hoped that employees would be inspired by each others work to increase the conception rate of new projects.

Before he started in on his sandwich, Owen conjured a sprite and instructed it to go explore the rest of the Main Facility. He programmed the sprite to make its way through the digital materials laboratory that was located on the floor directly below Laboratory 1. They were always doing something entertaining down there. Owen needed something interesting to relieve his thoughts of the endless stream of interviews his day had consisted of.

When Owen executed the procedures he had written for the sprite, it responded by slowly phasing through the floor. That was the quickest way for it to get down to the level below. Owen took his first bite of sauerkraut and corned beef on rye, as a screen showing what the projection saw materialized, floating at eye-level above his desk.

The researchers in the materials lab were responsible for how the digital objects reacted to each other. Different types of materials were constantly being analyzed for discrepancies between how they were modelled on the network and how they behaved in real life. Right now the scientists were attempting to refine the current models for rendering how plasma gas behaved when observed on the VIEW network.

This had become of particular importance because the popular AIR gaming channel, Alien Conquest, was using plasma rifles in its combat simulation. Many players had been complaining that the plasma bullets were glitching and that it was affecting the accuracy and immersivity of their gaming experience.

To better align the algorithms used in the plasma models on the network, Owen watched as the researchers attempted to reverse engineer the hologram of a real star. It was being projected into the facility via information collected from company observation telescopes in outer space. The giant representation of what was effectively millions of thermonuclear furnaces, burned in the middle of the enormous laboratory. It was surrounded by concentric fields of brightness filters to allow a true representation to be rendered in the room without blinding the researchers with the intensity of light it was producing.

It was obvious that the models were still a far way off the real thing. The coronal filaments that looped from the surface of the atomic sphere had discontinuous shapes. There were odd angular and spiralling arcs that could only have been artifacts of inefficient data structures within the code.

The mathematical physics behind plasma gas behaviour had been proven decades prior. Still, when all the equations were combined, the amount of data produced was still stifling by the standards of the day. The fusion and fission of the atoms inside the stellar orb were happening so rapidly that new collisions were occurring before the last reaction could be computed. These minute delays in the calculations were adding up to result in the bugs that were being experienced when plasma gases needed to be produced on the network.

Owen watched his projection watch the researchers work to resolve the problems with their rendition of the projected star. His intuition told him they weren't going to be able to make much progress without utilizing parallel computing methods. That would allow them to predict the potential outcomes of each reaction before it was affected by the multitude of other reactions going on around it.

Owen thought about how this just made a slew of new problems since you would have to make multiple predictions for each reaction and there were billions of reactions happening every instant. That many computations in tandem wouldn't be possible on a processor produced this millenium.

They were going to have to resort to some sort of statistical approach to approximate the outcomes of groups of reaction and establish threshold potentials for events to occur in a given region. It was going to be an interesting problem to see them solve once they had more time. The results were likely to have far reaching applications in the fields of data compression and parallel computation, both of which interested Owen deeply.

Owen's projection continued from the materials lab to the cultural lab where a group of researchers were reviewing historical records of footage from previous eras. They studied past ways, attempting to replicate the styles and fashions that were popular throughout history. It seemed that they had recently found a store of old analog footage from the 1960s that featured a previously un-rediscovered hairstyle that was unique to that era.

The researchers were studying footage of how women of that period were able to replicate the shape of a beehive with their hair. Owen could see from the footage that the secret seemed to be a copious amount of hair-glue to give the shape structure. He really hoped that once this unsightful style became available on the network that it didn't become very popular.

As he finished eating his lunch, Owen brought up his touch interface in order to dissolve his sprite. It was good to know that other projects weren't having the same difficulties his team was when it came to production bottlenecks. They weren't being targeted by terrorists though. It was time to find a new data compressor so that his team could get back to work.

Owen returned to the interview area just in time to see the back of an attractive young woman walking into the conference room. She must have been the next person applying for the position. He started to flip through the file about the young lady's employment history and was shocked when he saw the name on the file read, "Matilda Seiler." It couldn't be the same girl that he had met at the party last night. Could it?

She was there in person. Her thin figure was covered in a professional looking maroon pantsuit that made her seem more high-strung than the Mati that Owen had met the night before. Owen recalled that Mati's location had been set to L.A. when he had checked it that morning.

There was no time to do a network check to see if it was the girl that he had gotten security clearance to contact at Shayne's party. Not to mention the company would recuse him from interviewing her if they knew there was a possibility that they had met each other previously. Owen decided that the name must be common enough for it to just be a coincidence and began the interview as if he was meeting her for the first time.

"Hello, Ms. Matilda Seiler, is it?"

"Yes," she replied, "but everyone calls me Mati." If she was the same girl from the night before, she had decided to play the situation the same way as Owen.

"My name is Owen Lyonne, and I am an assistant lead on this Project. My father, the lead developer was unable to be here today to interview you."

"Sorry to hear that Mr. Lyonne, is your dad okay?"

"He's seen better days, but enough about that. Let's begin the interview process. I see in my notes that you attended Brussels Technical Academy and were a top software writer in your year."

"Yes, that's right. Then I went on to work in the Dubai Urban Settlement as the Software Lead on a Hardware project writing the programming for the latest generation of operating system for optical augments."

There was no longer any possibility that this was not the Matilda Seiler from last night. Originally from Brussels with ties to Dubai? Preferred to be called Mati? This was now too unique a profile for there to be an exact doppelganger anywhere else.

It was now plain to Owen that she hadn't altered her sprite's appearance all that much for the party. The hair colour was different, the real Mati was a redhead, but for the most part all of her facial features were identical to the features that her projection had displayed the night before.

These similarities hadn't been obvious to him until Owen had been certain it was her. They had been hidden by the fog of wishful thinking. She had clearly intended for Owen to figure it out. Without needing to say it, they both knew the other was in on the ruse.

The next portion of the interview went according to script and Mati was doing great. Her personality was refreshing and she already had some great ideas for how to get the data even more efficiently compressed than it was currently. She had been doing her homework and that sort of initiative was exactly what the team was looking for.

Owen would never admit it but it also certainly didn't hurt her chances that he found her so unbelievably cute. Their conversation was natural and almost too friendly for the importance of the situation. The interview took a turn however, when they reached the company imposed security questions.

"Do you ever think that it might be preferable to live a rural lifestyle?" Owen asked, in accordance with company requirements.

"All the time!" Mati replied, unaware of the grave error she had just made. Owen's face contorted into a grimace as he became unable to hide his disappointment. That was a sure fire way to be disqualified from the position. She had obviously gotten too comfortable with the circumstances in the light of their mutual insubordination,

"It's such a quaint existence for them isn't it. I often think about how those savages survive out there without the network. All the jealousy they must harbour. At the same time though, their heads aren't always caught up in the virtual realities that we in the cities are so busy getting lost in. Could you imagine the way your mind would wander without all the urban distractions? You'd really have to appreciate the real world around you if you couldn't just ignore it on the AIR channels."

Mati finally noticed that the expression on Owen's face had changed. "What's the matter Owen? Did I say something wrong?"

She had been rambling on, enjoying herself, feeling as if she was a shoo-in for the position. In his ears, Owen could already hear the company brass ordering him to end the interview.

A loyal employee would have answered how they were lucky to not have to live with the rural tribes. They would have expressed nothing but gratitude for everything the company gave to them and the technological advancements that they had access to. The company was not about to let some sort of ingrate get a job on their flagship project. Security was on their way to escort Ms. Seiler off the premises.

Owen let out a sigh, "That was the last thing you should have said. I'm sorry but we're going to have to stop the interview there. You should go wait outside."

"What?" Mati plead. The tears instantly welled in her eyes. "I thought I was doing fine. How does what I just said change anything?"

"Security officers are on their way to escort you from the property. I'm very sorry Mati, but there's nothing I can do." Owen had really been looking forward to giving her the job. "Please don't make this harder than it has to be."

"I just don't understand." Mati sobbed, as

some of her virtual makeup ran down her face. She collected her things and left the interview room not bothering to wait for security to show up.

Since their interview had ended so abruptly, Owen had quite a bit of time before his next appointment was scheduled. It was a good thing too. He needed to collect himself after what had just happened. Mati would have made a great addition to his team.

He thought about what went wrong and how things might have been different if he had been more honest. He should have indicated to the company that they had a previous history as soon as he was certain. His mind had been clouded by his feelings for her. Maybe if someone else would have been interviewing her she wouldn't have made such a absent minded error?

If she hadn't gotten so confident in there she would have seen through the intent of that question and given the answer the company had expected. There was no way that Owen would be allowed to give her the job now.

Chapter 5

There were only two more applicants to interview for the day. Compared to Mati, they just blended into the monotonous stream of candidates that Owen had already seen. More spectacular applicants with amazing recommendations. Nothing made any one of them stand out from the others. Owen wondered if he was going to have to just flip a coin to decide who got the job.

After the last interview, Owen went back to his office to look over the applicant's files and try and remember who had said what. The shock of what happened during Mati's interview had obviously affected how he had conducted himself during the rest. Owen couldn't decide if it put those applicants at an advantage or if it had hurt their chances.

He had felt distracted when he was with those lasy candidates. Maybe that had made Owen go easy on them? On the other hand, his preoccupation might have made him come across as distant and cold. That would have created unnecessarily tension. At this point, Owen was having trouble even remembering what either of them had said at all.

Luckily, the interviews were all recorded. Owen had also done his best to note each answer as it was given. He loaded these notes into the database and used the information to make a scoring chart program to help him sort through the applicants. Pictures of each of them were set against a race track backdrop that Owen pinned to stay attached to the wall in his office.

The board worked like a squirtgun midway game once found in the old carnivals. As he gave the chart various qualities that he was looking for in an applicant, the photos of better suited candidates progressed down the track.

While he was in the interview room, Owen had disabled all alerts from his profile. He thought it was extremely rude to the applicant to distract yourself with personal messages or bulletins. You were supposed to be talking to the person that you were actually in the room with. It was disheartening to be on the other end of that experience and Owen didn't want to upset a potential new hire before they had even started. Not that they were likely to get upset. Far too few people shared these sentiments and most people were used to constantly being ignored by those around them.

Opening the inbox for his messaging application, Owen found that he had over a dozen new messages. There are a few from Shayne, pictures and videos of some of the more debauturous moments from the night before. One message was from his dad. He wanted Owen to come straight home after work to have dinner and had ordered his favourite meal. Carter must have wanted something, it had been out of character for him recently to do anything nice without a reason. The rest of the messages were all from Mati.

Her first read, "How the hell did that happen? What did I do wrong? Call me." The timestamp indicated the message was sent only minutes after she had been escorted from the property.

This was the first definitive proof that the Mati from the party the night before and the Mati that had bombed her interview were one and the same. She had known the whole time during the interview. Owen hadn't changed his sprite's appearance in the least for the party.

He had worn khaki shorts that were partially covered by an oversized sleeveless t-shirt. The fabric of the shirt acted as a screen that displayed a microscopic view of various types of biochemical structures, like spontaneously assembling cytoskeletal structures or mitotically dividing embryos. His face and hair had been untouched. There was no way that she wouldn't have recognized him as soon as he'd entered the interview room.

It was probably a good thing that she hadn't passed the interview. Owen had been ready to give her the job but that might have been an irreversible mistake. If it had ever been found out that Owen hadn't reported that they had known each other before the interview he would be hauled in front of the board of ethics. His security clearance would be reduced to the point he couldn't work. Or worse. He could even be accused of intentionally subverting anti-terror measures and endangering the lives of his fellow employees. That meant banishment into the rural territories.

The rest of Mati's messages chronicled her realization of what exactly had gone wrong. "That was a security question wasn't it. How could I be so dumb?"

Another continued, "What was I thinking? Going on like that about the Subrurians during an interview. Especially for a job with the highest security clearance in the company." There were several more messages along these lines, in rapid fire. Her woe had gotten the better of her.

"Now I look like a rural sympathizer. It'll be years until I get over that reputation. Guess I should get ready to move into beta-tester housing."

"Why aren't you answering my calls. Do you have your alerts disabled? I don't have permission to check your network status."

"You must be in another interview. Please call me when you're done." Owen was reluctant. Why was Mati so eager to get in touch with him? There was nothing he could do at this point to get her the job. She had to know that. So what was the point in talking about it?

Maybe she wanted to continue where they had left off last night at the party? He knew he did. Owen decided that he would call her to find out. He was intrigued by her and not just because of her looks.

Owen wasn't worried about his calls and messages with Mati betraying their relationship. Active monitoring of the communication between employees only happened in extreme situations. Even further still an individual had to be notified if they had been flagged to be subjected to random call monitoring. All calls were of course recorded. For the most part, the contents of those records wouldn't so much as be glimpsed by the odd filtering algorithm.

It was not economical to waste network resources and processing capacity on superfluous measures. Also, public surveillance was very unpopular politically because it tended to shift the opinion of the electorate against otherwise sound campaign platforms. There was no way that another employee would ever be able to put together the conflict of interest to which Mati and he had both been party.

Owen was done work for the day and almost ready to leave. Before he arranged for a transport to take him home, he returned Mati's call. It only took two rings for the blank, blue golem to be replaced by a live projection of Mati. She had found time to reapply her digital mascara, not looking anywhere near as distraught as she had the last time Owen saw her.

"About time," She started. "I've been trying to get a hold of you since they kicked me off of the campus."

"Ya, I just saw that. I turned my alerts off while I was in the interviews."

"I guess that means you're a pretty old fashioned guy then, Owen. I don't know anyone that ever ignores calls anymore."

"I think its rude when people don't concentrate on the task at hand." Owen was almost regretting having called her back, he didn't want to have to explain himself. "Especially in an interview. How would you have liked it if I had spent our whole conversation typing messages to other people."

"But that's what everyone else does. It actually made me more uncomfortable that you weren't messaging during the interview. I thought it made our little ruse too obvious." This was the first time Owen and Mati openly discussed that they had done anything wrong. "It's good to know that's how you are with everyone."

"How far into the interview did you realize we knew each other?" Owen asked, trying to get the topic of conversation off of himself and back onto her.

"I knew who you were before the interview even started. I figured out who you were last night." Owen hadn't seen that coming.

Mati seemed to be a little more informed about the situation than he was. "Our sprite's didn't discuss it because your father was technically supposed to be giving the interview. I did my homework though. Your father hadn't conducted any of the interviews for the last five positions that were filled on the team. You did."

Owen began to suspect that he might be being manipulated. "How did you put all this together?"

"When we first arrived at the party and Shayne introduced you to me and Sarmad. I recognized your name immediately." She was at least trying to appear honest.

"Not to mention, its no secret that your fathers are close friends. My sprite was supposed to keep its distance to try and keep things professional, but when you came up and started hitting on me, you overrode my instructions."

"So, you didn't just tolerate my advances to try and get the job?" Owen didn't know if he should believe her. "This all seems a little too serendipitous to me. You're sure that you didn't go to that party looking for me?"

"Don't flatter yourself Owen," Mati was

getting flustered. "It's nothing like that. I've really enjoyed getting to know you. It did cross my mind this morning that our relationship might come up in the interview. I honestly wasn't sure if it was going to help my chances or hinder me."

"Well that question has been answered." Owen gave himself a little chuckle. Somethings are only ever obvious after the fact.

"I guess," Mati was not impressed at being the brunt of Owen's little joke. The situation had spiralled completely out of her control. "I probably wasn't going to be the one to get the job anyway. At least this way I don't have to wait to be disappointed."

"Are you kidding!?" Owen needed to make up for poking fun at her. "You're the only one all day that stood out. All the other applicants are dull and boring. I couldn't get them to open up at all in the interview. You, on the other hand, were friendly and engaging. You communicated on a real level, without straying from topic. It felt like you would have genuinely enjoyed working on the OtherObserver project; everyone else is just in it for the prestige."

"That's so nice of you to say Owen." Mati's sprite gave him a hug in return for his kind words.

"I was ready to give you the position before you were disqualified." Owen hugged Mati back and the two of them stood holding each other for a moment, standing in Owen's office.

They released their embrace, as Mati became only more disappointed with herself by this revelation. "Well I really fucked this all up then, didn't I?"

Mati's frustration was beginning to poke through. "Isn't there anything you can do Owen? Tell them that we knew each other before the interview and that's why I said what I did."

"Nothing would help, Mati." This was the part of the conversation that Owen had been dreading. "Telling them that would only get us both into trouble. Right now, you have nothing flagged on your profile. You've just been disqualified from this project. Security for each project is very specialized, since they all have different threats and susceptibilities. Our team has been experiencing a high degree of disappearances, or desertions, so they don't want anyone that sympathizes with the ruralites on the team. The security forces have decided that people with those ideals are more likely to be targets for rebel recruitment."

"So they think I'm going to be recruited by the rebels?"

"They don't go quite that far. It's just more likely enough that they don't want to take the chance. Like I said, this doesn't affect anything outside of this project. I really wish that I could hire you, I do, but there's nothing I can do."

"That's such bullshit, but I'm glad that they

keep their information to themselves." Mati was getting her temper back under control. "By the way. Why didn't you recuse yourself in the interview today. A good company boy like yourself shouldn't be breaking the rules like that. Didn't you recognize my name?"

"I've been asking myself that all afternoon." Owen had no idea what the answer was. "I had myself convinced that it wasn't you. I thought it was just too big a coincidence. I didn't even recognize you definitively until we started going into your education and employment history. Your hair was different last night. I wish I had reported our relationship though. It seems like if someone else had interviewed you, you might still have a shot at the job."

"No. It's my fault Owen. That was obviously a security question and our relationship had nothing to do with my answer." Mati had now accepted that things couldn't be changed. She had to pick herself up and keep going. "I've always let my mouth get me into trouble."

"It's still too bad. What will you do now? Is there any other work for you to apply for here in LA?" Owen had a vested interest in this question. If Mati moved away, their relationship would be much less physical than it could be otherwise. "Or would you rather try somewhere else?

"Well," Mati started. She had noticed that when Owen asked if she would stay, he got a little glimmer in his eye and his grin got a little wider. "I do have this one project in town here that I might be able to use your help on."

"Oh, what would that be?" Owen didn't know it but at this point he would have done almost anything to get her to stay.

"Ummm. First, I wanted to ask you about something. It's pretty personal, but if we're going to be spending more time together we should get to know each other better."

"We're going to be spending more time together, are we?" Owen was elated. "I think I'd like that. Ask away."

"Okay. I noticed that you really don't have many augments compared to Shayne. I thought that was strange. Weren't both your parents on the team that was attacked developing that technology? Why haven't you got more like him? He said last night at the party that his augments are a tribute to both your parents' legacies. Do you not agree?"

"Wow, that is personal." Owen was shocked that she had even thought to ask something that went so deep into the root of himself. He would never answer a question like that to someone he had met in the last twenty-four hours, but there was something about Mati that Owen couldn't resist.

"Well," Owen continued, trying to find the right words to express the feelings he had been secretly harbouring for years. "I guess the main reason I don't have as many augments as Shayne would be that we think about them entirely differently. He and I don't exactly see our parents' legacy the same way. He is under the impression that the augments themselves are what our parents contributed to society. In his perspective the rebels and their attack were the only things responsible for our parents' death. This is, of course, the official story and no one in the company would ever deny that those are the facts of what happened that day."

Owen paused. For just moment, he second guessed his reasoning for sharing these secrets with a practical stranger. "But, I can't shake this feeling in the pit of my stomach that it was actually the augments that were responsible for our parent's death. Not directly. But, it might have been the idea of them that drove the rebels to attack. What if the company hadn't been pushing such a flashy, controversial project? Maybe then the Neoluddites wouldn't have been forced to resort to such extreme measures."

As Mati listened to Owen say this, her face slowly tightened into a grin. "That's kind of how I thought you might feel. Would you say that you mistrust technology?"

Owen had to think hard about this one. He loved using digital devices and spent all of his time connected to the VIEW network. He must trust technology, but just not completely. "I think new technology needs to be properly integrated with society for it to be safe. If aspects of a new technology are left ununderstood the social effects can be devastating."

"You are the guy to help me then. It'll be fun to work together. Meet me at midnight in the Gamers' Park near the Hilltop Employee Residences. I know a secluded place where we won't be disturbed."

"I'll already be there playing the AIR channels with Shayne. I can just come over to you when it's time." Owen thought about how caught up into his game he could get. "I better make sure to set an alarm so I don't geek out and miss you."

"Okay. I'll message you more details about the exact location in a little bit. See you later tonight." Mati's sprite reached in and gave Owen a kiss on the cheek.

"Uhh," Owen was taken aback by Mati's unsolicited affection. Not that he was complaining about it. "Right. Tonight at midnight. Wherever you say. Good bye."

"Good b-." Mati was so quick to end the call that the end of her words were cut off as her sprite vanished from Owen's office.

Owen notified his driver that he was ready to go and the transport was waiting for him when he walked out of the Main Facility. On the ride home Owen reviewed the files on the job applicants trying to figure out how he was going to choose between them. He tried to remember what his initial impression of each one had been, thinking that might give him some insight he had otherwise overlooked. Owen didn't like how subjective this process was becoming.

The transport dropped him off safely in front of his building. Owen took the stairs up to the apartment he and his father shared on the third floor. Inside, he found Carter busily working in the dining room with a guest. He had invited an old friend over to help him work on a side project. Shayne's father, Seymour Riche, had been coming over to help Carter more often lately. Even if he had died in that blast almost ten years ago.

The Telexistence system, that ran on the VIEW network, created comprehensive profiles of every employee. These profiles chronicled every aspect of the user's life so that their behaviours could be accurately predicted for any given situation. This information served as the brain for the projected sprites that acted as the user's virtual representatives in situations that they were unable to physically attend. These profiles were continuously updated as the individuals experienced new events which informed their decisions in novel ways.

At some point around twenty years ago, the Telexistence profiles got so good at simulating realistic representations of the users that sprites became able to continue living for people after they'd died. Seymour Riche was now a spirit, as sprites of the dead had come to be called. His projection had been aged appropriately, so it looked ten years older than the real 'Uncle' Seymour that Owen remembered from his childhood.

"Hello Mr. Riche," Owen greeted the spirit of his father's best friend, who also happened to be his best friend's father. He gave no attention to his own dad. "Did you spend the whole day working on that side project again?"

"Yes we sure did. I think we're almost done. We just have to smooth out her personality traits and work on how to integrate new memories. You must be so excited," replied Seymour. Owen wasn't, but he didn't care to share this fact.

"Thank you again Owen for covering for me at work," chimed in Carter. He didn't pay any notice to the fact his son hadn't acknowledged him. "I'm sorry that it's becoming such a regular occurrence."

"Whatever dad. I'm getting used to it." It had been a long day for Owen and he was a little harsher than he meant to be.

"You should be nicer to your father Owen," Seymour chastised him for his tone. "His mind is so preoccupied with what we are doing here that he probably wouldn't be able to focus at work anyway."

"That's not an excuse." Owen was worried about how their secret project was affecting his father's mind. "If that's the case maybe you guys should give it a break for a little while. She'll still be there when you go back to it."

"We're too close for that to be an option!" Carter said this with such authority in his voice that there was no point for Owen to argue. "We'll have her back before you know it."

Today the use of the Telexistence system was so widespread in the urban centers that its was rare for anyone to pass on without leaving a spirit behind to represent them in the afterlife. This was not the case a decade earlier. Seymour had projected himself enough while he was alive to have developed his profile to the point that he could persist as a spirit. Unfortunately Carter and Seymour's wives, Avery and Hudson, had not been so lucky.

The surviving pair had spent most of the last decade scouring the network for any trace of Avery Lyonne. They were going to compile all of the digital memories of her to rebuild her Telexistence profile and resurrect a spirit of her. Owen even got recruited into the project as a beta-tester. He was supposed to give them feedback on how their current version of his dead mother could be improved.

"How was your day at the office Owen?" Seymour asked, to break the silence after Carter had ended the last subject.

"It was fine, there really wasn't much going on. If I didn't have to do the interviews I would have had nothing to do."

"Well at least covering for me didn't keep you

from anything." Carter was trying his best to put a positive spin on things.

"I guess. I did look in on the trial run of the current software. It seems like we are having some success at achieving simultaneous experiences. They seem to be limited to a single sense at a time currently though. Reliably at least."

"That's a great result. I'll be happy to report that to the company tomorrow."

"The results of the trial have already been submitted to Project Supervision." Owen was glad to quash his father's sense of entitlement.

"Alright then," Carter was good at hiding his disappointment. "Excellent work then son."

"Ya Owen, you did great." Seymour interjected himself into the conversation. "It seems like it's about time for me to get going though. I have to be getting to a party rally in Washington."

"Are you sure you can't stay for tonight's tests?" Carter attempted to twist his friend's arm.

"Carter, I can't," Seymour had obviously already explained this to his friend. "I can only have three sprites active at once. If they aren't all at the rally people might think that I have something more important to be doing. We don't want people to start asking questions about what were doing. Resurrection isn't exactly on the level."

It had taken people long enough to get used to the idea of spirits being left behind. The thought of going back and making spirits of people that had been dead for years would take magnitudes longer for the masses to accept. Even worse, the thought might provoke segments of the population to leave the cities, just as the invention of spirits had near the end of the Second Dark Ages.

"Okay good friend. I'll see you soon then. Expect a message from me later about how the testing goes tonight."

"I'd like that very much. Good night Owen. I hear you and Shayne are meeting for some games later. Will you two be sending sprites to the rally?"

"I will be for sure, Mr. Riche. I've been looking forward to it."

"Very good then. Okay, Goodbye." And his spirit disappeared in a white glow of light. That was really the only thing that differentiated a sprite from a spirit. Sprites had a blue aura, spirits were white. NPC characters in the AIR games tended to flash red or green, but they could be customized to be of any colour or none at all. Left alone with his father, Owen became anxious for a reason to excuse himself.

"So, dinner should be here any moment Owen." His father tried to engage his son in conversation. "I was going to boot up your mother and see how she did in a family dinner atmosphere."

"Sounds great," Owen fibbed. He started heading out of the room. "I'm going to go have a shower before dinner."

"But won't you stay and say hi to your mother?" Carter's request wasn't heard. Owen was already halfway down the hall.

When Owen returned from washing he found his incompletely resurrected mother waiting for him at the dining room table. Unlike real spirits, Avery hadn't aged a day since her death. In fact, since most of the data that Seymour and Carter had found of her was from before her death, she seemed a little younger than she was when she died. All of the information they had found was blended together to create the weighted average of her entire digitized history in order to represent her once again. Seeing her instantly gave Owen a sinking feeling deep in his stomach that he was sure would ruin his appetite.

Owen took his spot at the dinner table, at the opposite end from where his father would be sitting. His mother's spirit stared straight ahead waiting for something to respond to. Her present behavioural algorithms were not able to initiate a conversation, she could only do anything if someone else said something or made a specific gesture. Owen was happy that he didn't have to interact with her yet.

His father walked in from the kitchen with plates of steak dinner and announced. "Dinner time!"

Owen wondered if his dad hadn't specifically preprogrammed Avery's projection to wait for those exact words, because as soon as they registered in the logic of her programming she came to life. "Oh goody! What are we having tonight darling?" She exclaimed with excitement.

"Steak and potatoes for the men," Carter answered, as he passed Owen his plate. Once he had delivered what he was holding, another plate materialized in Carter's hand. A digital meal for a digital person. "I thought you might like salmon and rice, honey. I hope the fish is fresh."

It was all a little too phoney for Owen. Aside from a few common courtesies, he spent most of the dinner muted. Carter was too busy getting lost in the illusion of his wife's resurrection to notice his son's lack of engagement.

Owen choked back tears as his parents reminisced together about all of the memories that Carter had been able to preload into Avery's profile. Whenever Carter would ask too intimate a detail about an event, it would trigger an error in Avery's programing. If she couldn't remember aspects properly, but knew she ought to be able to, the shock would cause her spirit to skip.

These errors were the worst to watch. Avery's face would pull into the deepest grimace it was capable of. Her awareness of the discontinuity of her own memory caused her so much despair she would sometimes let out a scream that would curdle the blood of even the most savage of predators. Her proceduralized behaviours would stall as well, causing her image to flicker and her movement to jerk and twitch.

The only way for Carter to fix the bug was to restart her projection. The third time it happened, Owen had to excuse himself to the kitchen. He took his half empty plate and got a glass of water to try and calm his nausea. To Owen's dismay, his father followed him to the kitchen, stopping first only to reboot Avery. Carter entered the room, already speaking, just as Owen was taking his first sip from the glass.

"There are definitely still a few bugs to work out when she gets caught up in a memory. But it's a lot better, right?" Carter was giddy. As far as he's concerned his wife was back from the dead. "She's really almost back!"

"I'm not so sure dad. Seems like there's a long way to go before the mom I remember." Owen still felt sick from seeing the contorted face that his mother's projection had made. He tried desperately to change the subject. "Are you going to be able to make it into work tomorrow or what?"

"You know," snarled Carter. He wasn't going to take that kind of disrespect from his son any longer. "I'm sick of the lack of enthusiasm that you're showing about this. I've almost brought back your mother. Aren't you happy? After all these years and we almost have her back with us."

"That doesn't mean that we can ignore our other responsibilities dad. They're going to start getting suspicious about why you're missing so much time at your real job."

"Fuck them! Just wait 'til they see her when I'm done."

"Is that so, dad? Is what you're doing even legal? How would they react if they knew that you were bringing her back from the dead?" Owen knew that this was a sensitive subject.

There were no rules on the books regarding this matter, but the current social climate didn't make resurrection likely to be all that well received. There was a fair bit of skepticism regarding the mental effects on family members that interacted with ghosts of deceased loved ones. If Carter was found out, he would certainly be sent for psychological evaluation.

Carter became irate. "Well, fuck you too then!" He yelled loudly at Owen while storming off to his bedroom.

Carter had left the mess from dinner behind in the dining room, as well as Avery's spirit sitting at the table. Witnessing the fight had caused her projection to go all buggy again.

Owen checked the time on his clock interface. It was just about time to meet Shayne and work on their Medieval Fantasy characters. He doubted that his father would leave his room the rest of the night and he didn't want the place to smell when he got back. He pretended that the imitation of his mother wasn't there while he cleaned. She just sat there watching him, unable to communicate without his lead, flickering every once and a while. It hadn't been a bad glitch this time.

When the space had been set right, Owen went to his room to get warmer thermal garments. It was getting dark and the temperature was dropping. It sucked to be cold when you were playing the AIR channels. The chill ruined the realism and immersivity of the digital experience.

The final chore he had before Owen left the apartment was to pull up his console interface to patch into the Telexistence profile editor. His dad had customized the normal editor so that he could do more complex things with it. Like resurrecting the profiles of the dead, for instance. From the editor Owen was able to shut Avery's projection off. The last thing he wanted was for her to still be sitting there skipping when he got back.

...to be continued in Episode 2, available soon.